Murder on the Dancefloor

A Patricia Fisher Mystery

Book 6

Steve Higgs

Text Copyright © 2019 Steven J Higgs

Publisher: Steve Higgs

The right of Steve Higgs to be identified as author of the Work has been asserted by him in accordance with the Copyright, Designs and Patents Act 1988

All rights reserved.

The book is copyright material and must not be copied, reproduced, transferred, distributed, leased, licensed or publicly performed or used in any way except as specifically permitted in writing by the publishers, as allowed under the terms and conditions under which it was purchased or as strictly permitted by applicable copyright law. Any unauthorised distribution or use of this text may be a direct infringement of the author's and publisher's rights and those responsible may be liable in law accordingly.

'Murder on the Dancefloor' is a work of fiction. Names, characters, businesses, organisations, places, events and incidents either are the product of the author's imagination or are used fictitiously. Any resemblance to actual persons, living or dead, events or locations is entirely coincidental.

Table of Contents:

- Quite the Man
- Champagne Reception
- The Show Can't Go On
- A Mystery to Solve
- Clues
- Reinforcements
- Smoking Gun
- Accusations
- A Challenge
- Gin
- Where's Rajesh?
- The Morgue
- Mystery Solved
- A Pattern
- Vihaan Veghale
- Lies
- Trickster
- Research
- Mrs Patel
- The Patels
- In Custody
- What It is All About
- Murder
- Number Three
- Confession
- Final Clue

The Big Reveal

Secret Mission

Breakfast in Bed

Epilogue:

Author Note:

Extract from Mission for the Maharaja

Unwelcome Intruder

Banquet

Zombie Granny

Rochester High Street - Saturday 23rd October 1155hrs

Quite the Man

The sun was setting to starboard as the Aurelia gracefully churned away from Chennai. Our two-night stay had been as wonderful and exotic as one might expect but it would remain forever indelibly etched in my memory for one particular reason. That reason was the man currently walking arm in arm with me as we promenaded along the top deck.

Captain Alistair Huntley was a handsome man of fifty-four. He was intelligent and successful, gregarious but also reserved and to the list of attributes I already counted, I was now able to add that he was a gentle and wonderful lover. Before we arrived in Chennai, he surprised me with an invitation to join him at the Leela Palace Hotel, a brand new and ultra-modern hotel on the seafront. He had champagne delivered to the room, the honeymoon suite no less, and we stayed in there for many hours on that first night, ordering room service rather than getting dressed to go out for food.

Now we were back onboard the Aurelia and our relationship, which until now had been something he wished to remain private, was well and truly out in the open. Foolishly, my paranoia had been telling me he was somehow ashamed of me and that was why he was so reluctant to make our relationship public. That concern was long gone as he introduced me to everyone we met.

We reached the prow of the ship where dozens of passengers were gathered, and crew members were serving champagne to those who wanted to toast their voyage. The captain needed to do nothing more than flick his eyebrows at the steward with the drinks and two glasses of fine bubbly came our way.

'Thank you, Giles.' Alistair shot the steward a smile. I found it remarkable that he not only knew the name of over a thousand crew members, but he also seemed to know most of the passengers by name as well. He drifted through the crowd, waving at people and shaking hands. He stopped to congratulate a young couple on their marriage which had apparently occurred earlier today, and he introduced me to everyone as if having me on his arm was something to brag about.

He made my heart swell.

I noted that he only sipped his champagne, barely imbibing any of it because he had work to do yet tonight.

'I'm afraid I will have to go soon, Patricia.' He turned to face me and took both my hands in his. 'There is much that I must oversee. My new deputy is vastly experienced and ought to be a captain himself already, but he is new to the ship and new to my crew. It would be wrong of me to test him too severely on his second day.'

'And you have a live event being televised tonight,' I replied.

He smiled a rueful smile. 'Yes, I do like to make my life complicated. Not that I had a lot of choice, you understand. These decisions are made far higher up the chain than the mere captain of a ship.'

The event we talked about was a live edition of *Stars that Dance* which was being filmed in the ship's top deck restaurant which even now was having finishing touches applied as the crew of the ship and the staff of the show converted it into a ballroom for the event. The restaurant had a glass ceiling and walls which they intended to utilise to provide a star-filled backdrop for the live event. It was the biggest show on Indian television with half the country tuning in each week.

The dancers and the celebrities were already on board of course. They arrived two days ago to begin settling in. The stars were all housed in suites on the top deck while the less famous dancers and crew for the show itself were a few decks below. The host, a famous Bollywood star in his seventies called Irani Patel was my new neighbour in one of the plushest suites on the ship.

At my feet, my little Dachshund, Anna, tugged her lead and yipped a warning bark as a man approached us. I looked up to see that it was Lieutenant Baker, a member of the ship's security team and someone I had grown quite fond of.

He saluted Alistair crisply. 'Sir, might I beg a moment of your time?'

Alistair was instantly alert, his mind back on his job and he let go my hand as he said, 'Report.'

Lieutenant Baker cut his eyes to me as if asking Alistair if I should be involved but proceeded anyway. 'Another break in has been reported, sir. This time it is Mr Patel's suite.'

Alistair's top lip twitched in annoyance. Then, seeing my curious expression, he explained. 'This started two weeks ago. People reporting that someone has been in their suite. Nothing gets taken but a calling card is left. Whoever is behind it is taunting us.'

My brow furrowed. 'They leave a calling card?'

'Yes, quite literally. They leave a business card on the nightstand each time. It has a signature on it below a stylised stroke from a paint brush.'

Lieutenant Baker reached into his jacket pocket. 'I have one here, sir.' He handed it to Alistair who showed it to me. In a small evidence bag was a plain white piece of card with a black signature below a swish of red paint. Alistair turned it around to show the other side was blank.

Alistair turned his attention back to his lieutenant. 'Has Mr Patel confirmed all his belongings are still present?'

'I have Bhukari and Pippin with him now, sir. They were going through his suite and attempting to find anything that might have been disturbed. He was hopping mad, sir.'

Alistair nodded at the news. I didn't know the host though I was given to understand there wasn't a person in India who didn't know him. His face was centre stage of the posters displayed about the ship, a beaming smile beneath kindly eyes.

The live event was in just a few hours and thanks to Alistair I had a prime seat next to him. Alistair clearly needed to go, and I needed to get changed and ready for the event, so I gave Anna's lead a quick tug to get her attention. 'Time to go, little girl.' She stared up at me and tilted her head as if trying to understand what I was telling her.

Alistair offered me his elbow. 'I'll walk down with you. I want to see the issue with Mr Patel's suite for myself.' Ahead of us, Baker turned around and started back the way he had come, weaving through the crowd of passengers enjoying the early evening sunshine. His passing cleared a route through for us which was a good thing because Anna liked to tangle people with her lead if she could.

As we walked, I was puzzling over why someone would break into a cabin just to leave a card. I asked Alistair about it. 'When did this start?'

'That's actually hard to be sure about,' he replied. 'The first time it was reported was just after we left Hawaii. The passenger reported that someone had been in his room. It was after the cleaner had done their rounds so there was no reason for there to be anyone from the crew accessing his cabin. Once alerted to it and in possession of the first card, it wasn't long before the security team were able to confirm that other passengers had also found them. Every time, the card is left on the right-hand nightstand, and it is always the suites on the top deck. A thorough search always reveals that nothing has been taken. It is perplexing.'

'Perplexing,' I repeated. 'It's certainly that. How many cabins so far?'

'Seventeen that we know of.' We reached the doors, which Lieutenant Baker was holding open for us, and passed into the shade inside. The top deck restaurant was just to our left where we could see all manner of activity taking place. The countdown to the show was under two hours now and dozens of people - television crew and those involved in setting up the live transmission, were scurrying about performing various complex tasks. A blast of music made me jump as it caught me by surprise. Anna barked in response, undoubtedly also startled by it.

Alistair was escorting me to my suite, but our route would take us to Patel's suite first. It also took us right in front of the door to the top deck gymnasium, which opened just as we got to it, my good friend, Barbie, emerging right in front of us.

She beamed her smile at us. 'Hello, sir. Hi, Patty. Are you all set for the big event tonight?' We didn't slow down as we passed the gym door, so she fell into step with us along the passageway.

Alistair said, 'Good evening, Miss Berkeley. Am I right that you were one of the lucky crew members to get a ticket for tonight?'

'Yes, I was,' she gushed. 'I was so excited when they drew my name. I never win anything.' There had been a draw for attendance because the seats in the audience were limited. Most of the seats went to passengers but the captain offered fifty tickets to the crew as well. I was going as the captain's guest and would be sat right next to the panel of judges, but I was glad Barbie got to go as well. Her ball gown was already hanging in one of my spare bedrooms as we planned to get ready together. We had known the event was coming and went shopping in one of the exquisite boutiques on the eighteenth deck a few days ago. My ball gown was stupidly expensive and I hadn't been able to decide between two of them so had bought both, arguing with myself about returning one or both of them ever since.

The three of us turned the next corner which took us into the passageway that contained the entrance to my suite but there was a commotion ahead of us.

'Get out!' The shout came from inside the Montgomery Suite. It was the second largest suite on the ship and the one next door to mine. It was also the one in which the show's host, Irani Patel, was staying and I felt certain the heavily accented voice was his.

Young Lieutenant Pippin was standing in the passageway before us looking both embarrassed and harassed. The door to the suite was open in front of him and I could hear the voice of Lieutenant Bhukari coming from within the suite.

'Sir, I need to take the card as evidence.'

'I'm afraid not, young lady. I intend to keep it as my own evidence. This cruise line, the security team that you represent, have failed me. I have priceless items in this cabin, and someone has broken in to steal them.'

'Is anything missing, sir?'

Before the man inside could answer the question, we arrived at his open door and Alistair went straight inside. 'Good evening, sir.' Alistair exuded an air of utter confidence, it made him look like he belonged to be wherever he was. I saw him approach the smaller, elderly Indian gentleman and extend his hand in a way that guaranteed the other man would accept it. 'Captain Alistair Huntley at your service. I understand someone broke into your suite this evening. This is most embarrassing for me and indeed Purple Star Cruise Lines. On behalf of the entire crew, I offer my most heartfelt apology that you should have suffered in this way.'

Somewhat placated by Alistair's humble apology, Irani Patel lowered his tone when he spoke. 'Thank you, Captain. I am however concerned that my privacy has been invaded and my belongings stolen. Then he flicked a wrist to push his shirt beyond his suit sleeve. A cufflink shone, a deep blue catching the light in an iridescent way. When he saw Alistair look at them, he said, 'They were a gift from the Sultan of Brunei. I performed at his fiftieth birthday party. They are priceless blue opals, some of the rarest gems on the planet. Now you understand why I am sensitive about protecting my possessions?'

Alistair inclined his head as if agreeing. 'Lieutenant Bhukari is here to assist in determining if anything is missing and to ensure your suite is safe. She will arrange to provide you with new keycards once the lock has been inspected and the code for it changed.'

'Yes, Captain, that all sounds very efficient but my wife has been terrified by this event.' I saw him indicate with his arm but had to move position to be able to see the person he referred to. A mousy, plain woman in traditional Indian dress stood a few feet behind her husband. She was looking down at the floor when she said, 'I will be fine, Irani.'

Mr Patel looked displeased with his wife's response, but he turned to her and patted her shoulder, a show of affection and concern. Then, over his shoulder he said, 'I have too little time to deal with this now, Captain. I have a live performance to prepare for and most of India about to tune in to watch me. I must prepare. I will keep the card though and let you know if I believe anything has been taken. I am just glad my cufflinks are safe.'

Alistair gestured for Deepa Bhukari to leave the cabin ahead of him. 'My crew will be on hand when you are ready for them, Mr Patel. Good luck tonight.' Then he too left the cabin and closed the door behind him.

Lieutenant Bhukari was waiting for her captain. 'Sir, I think he plans to put in a false claim against the cruise line for his belongings being stolen.'

I shook my head to clear it, surprised at what Bhukari had just said. 'I thought no one had reported anything stolen previously.'

'I don't think anything was stolen this time either,' she replied. 'He started making up a list of missing items like a diamond necklace and diamond earrings, claiming they had been in a drawer and not in the safe where he showed us the rest of his jewellery. I think he was lying.'

Alistair interrupted. 'I think we should discuss this later. Until then, please go about your duties. I must return to the bridge.' He was speaking to me now. 'I will meet you at the champagne reception at seven thirty?'

'Yes.' I spared him a smile though it felt out of place with the shouting and accusations. He kissed my hand and started on his way to the bridge. Pippin and Bhukari took their leave also, leaving Barbie and me in the passageway alone. Barbie was visibly itching to get on with the party preparation portion of our evening.

I shot her a smile and started in the direction of my suite. 'I think I know something that will get us in the mood.' The something I knew were my good friends, gin and tonic. There just happened to be some chilled bottles of tonic in my suite and a bottle of Hendricks gin in the freezer.

I swiped my card against the door of my suite and pushed it open. Jermaine appeared in my central living space of the suite before Barbie and I could get inside and close the door behind us. My tall, strong, and very capable Jamaican butler was always at hand to serve me day or night and often went with me when I went ashore. I had been on board for seven weeks now and thought of him as a very dear friend. A recent brush with a deadly disease had weakened him but he was almost back to full strength and insisted he was ready for active duty.

'Good evening, madam, Barbie.' He was very rigid in performing his butler's duties and insisted on addressing me as Madam no matter what the occasion.

'Hello, Jermaine,' I replied. 'Can you fix us a couple of drinks, please?'

'Very good, madam.' He turned on the spot and walked slowly back to the kitchen area at the far end of my open plan living room.

I let Anna off her lead whereupon she immediately bounded across the room, jumped onto the couch and curled up in a ball. She eyed me lazily with her chin over her tail, daring me to have another task for her. Then, satisfied, she closed her eyes.

It was pretty much the last moment of calm that night.

Champagne Reception

The pre-event reception was for a very small group of VIP guests which once again included me because I was dating the captain. Unfortunately, it didn't include Barbie but she seemed fine with that, remaining in my suite to continue getting ready and chatting amiably with Jermaine as I left.

A steward offered me a glass on the way in which I took for the look it gave rather than to drink. I wanted my head clear and the gin and tonic I already drank an hour ago was quite enough alcohol to dull my senses. I had on the tallest pair of high heels I had ever worn and had some concern that I might fall over in them. I was feeling brave when I bought them in the Philippines, my inner Imelda speaking to me when I tried them on. It hadn't helped that I was with Barbie and she was trying on similar shoes and looking amazing in them. It also hadn't helped that I had imbibed two industrial strength gin and tonics with lunch before we went shoe shopping, but hey ho.

Alistair wanted to escort me from my suite but I knew how much he already had to fit into this evening so I insisted I would find him there. He was easy to spot as he was tall, and his white uniform stood out among the brightly clothed dancers in their incredibly tight costumes. It was also easy to pick out the pairs of dancers as each costume had a male and a female offering though it was less easy to pick out which were the professional dancers, and which were the celebrities. This was because some of the celebrities had very lean, athletic bodies much like the dancers. Others though stood out. An older woman in her sixties with a shock of grey hair wore a ballroom gown designed for a woman in her twenties though I had to concede that she wore it well. An overweight man sweating in his tuxedo had to be the celebrity half of his duo and there were a couple of others I suspected to be the celebrity rather than the dancer simply because of their age.

I had never watched the show, not even the English version, but I understood the basic format. They perform a different dance each week and are judged on their ability, then voted for by the at-home audience. Each week the pool of celebrities is whittled down until one is crowned champion for that season.

Alistair saw me come in and risked a quick wave. I waved back but he was all the way across the room and in conversation with a group of passengers and show stars already. I would make my way to him, but I spied a table of nibbles and made my way to them first. I was hungry.

There were others already there, picking over the bite-sized morsels. Among them were a dancing couple, and they were arguing.

'I'm just going to have a few bites to keep me going,' protested the woman. I hadn't seen her until now, but she was clearly the celebrity half of her duo simply because she wasn't stick-thin. She was actually a bit plump and the gauzy, skin-tight dress wasn't doing her any favours.

Her male counterpart was trying to move her away from the food. 'Taginda, you know the nutritionist wants you to only eat the food he recommends. If I am going to perform lifts with you in the later stages of the competition, you have to lose weight.'

She rounded on him and he took a step back. 'Did you just call me fat?' she snarled.

The man cast his eyes down. 'No. No, definitely not. I just need you to weigh less if you want me to lift you.'

'Maybe you need to get a little stronger. Here, have one of the these pakoras to bulk you up; they're yummy.' She then shoved the triangular parcel at his mouth and might have crushed it into his face if a different dancer hadn't stepped in between them.

'That's enough, Taginda, leave Rajesh alone. Besides, you are fat.' The new girl was taller by several inches than Taginda and made a point of staring down at her. She also possessed the perfect dancer's body most women would kill for.

Taginda wasn't cowed though. As the new girl turned away, she grabbed a handful of her ornate hair and yanked it. All around the buffet table, there were gasps as the passengers and other dancers backed away. 'Just because he's sleeping with you doesn't mean he's not gay, Dayita. You look like you could use a snack too.' Then she shoved the pastry into Dayita's open mouth.

Two more dancers grabbed Taginda just as she let go of the taller woman's hair. Dayita had been pulled off balance and was choking on the pakora as she tried to right herself. Then she fell, her foot slipping on a piece of loose pakora that had fallen to the deck and she tumbled with a shout of pain.

'My lord, what's going on here?' asked Irani Patel, the show's host, as he too arrived. 'Dayita are you alright?' He looked genuinely concerned and his face was angry when he swung it back to stare at Taginda. 'Taginda, what did you do?'

She finished chewing and swallowed. 'Why are you bothering with her? What about me? I'm the star of this show.'

Irani Patel got to his feet, carefully handing Dayita over to Rajesh to look after. 'Taginda, you have no right...'

'He called me fat,' snapped Taginda. 'And she got in my face one time too many. Why have I got to be partnered with her gay boyfriend?'

'I'm not gay!' argued Rajesh. He was kneeling on the deck with Dayita next to him. She was trying to get up but wincing in pain each time she moved. 'I think you've really hurt her,' he said, glancing up at Taginda.

'Good. Serves her right for calling me fat,' replied Taginda as she popped another piece of food in her mouth.

'It's my knee,' wailed Dayita. 'I can't put any weight on it.' She looked to be in pain and when she lifted the hem of her dress, we could all see her right knee was swelling. She shot a hateful look at Taginda. 'You horrible fat troll. I'm going to kill you for this.'

Taginda laughed. 'Ha! I'd like to see you try. My left arm weighs more than you.'

The show's host finally found some gumption and started to assert himself. 'Taginda, that's enough!' he roared. Then, more calmly, 'I think we all need to take a breath. We need to get someone to look at Dayita's knee, that's the first priority.' Then he turned his gaze toward the offensive woman. 'Taginda, you need to learn some humility before someone teaches you a terrible lesson.' It sounded like a threat and his eyes were filled with malice as if she had insulted him personally somehow.

Dayita's partner, or at least a man wearing an outfit that matched hers, appeared next to me. 'Whatever has happened?' he asked as he pushed through the crowd.

Dayita looked up at him and pointed at her aggressor. 'That fat troll tried to kill me. She's had the popular vote because people feel sorry for the fat girl trying to dance but she sees you and me as her competition. She wanted me out of the way.'

'Can you still dance?' he asked, and I could hear the desperate plea in his voice. She lifted her dress again to show him her knee and he turned his gaze to the show's host. 'Irani, how can she dance tonight? What does that mean for the competition?'

The host sighed. 'It will be treated the same as a training incident. Dayita cannot dance but if she can recover by next week you can simply be discounted this week. If Dayita's injury is worse than that then we bring in another dancer for you.'

The man looked concerned not relieved though. 'Discounted this week? What does that mean?'

Irani cocked an eyebrow and I got a sense that Dayita's partner was pretty but a little dumb. 'It means you get a free pass for this week. You won't dance, so you cannot be voted off.'

Taginda spluttered, bits of food flying from her mouth as she did. 'What? How's that fair?'

'Nevermind that!' raged Dayita from the deck. 'What are you going to do about her? She attacked me. She needs to be disqualified.'

Irani wasn't happy when he next spoke. He rubbed his forehead and sighed again. 'I can't disqualify her. We cannot afford to lose two couples from the show tonight. The competition has ten more weeks to run. We have eleven couples left. If anyone leaves the competition, we will run a short season and the network will never allow it.'

'And I'm the one getting the most votes each week,' added Taginda. 'If I go, I'll tell everyone it was because of you, Dayita. What will life be like when the whole of India hates you?' she finished with a gloating smile of satisfaction.

'That's enough, Taginda!' snapped Irani.

Two members of crew from the top deck aid station arrived at a run. They had a stretcher between them which they could have used to barge through the people formed around Dayita, but their shouts were sufficient to part the crowd.

As they began to administer to Dayita, I drifted away. As I moved, I turned but having not looked behind me, I bumped straight into a man, my feet tangled in his and we both pitched over onto the floor.

'Goodness,' said a muffled voice from somewhere under my left armpit. I was trying to right myself without having to put my hands on him, but he was beneath me and all the extra material from my ball gown was getting in the way. I tried to get up but my stupid heel caught in something and I heard a tear of material.

Mercifully, Alistair arrived to offer me his hand. Finally back on my feet and glowing red with embarrassment, I saw the poor man I had flattened. 'I'm so sorry. I am such a clutz. Are you alright?'

The gentleman was wearing a dinner jacket as were all the men who were not dancers or members of crew. He accepted Alistair's hand up and spared me a smile. 'I will be fine, my dear. I have to say it's been a while since a woman wrestled me to the floor. I rather enjoyed it.' The man was ninety if he was a day and he grinned cheekily at me. His suit fit him poorly, his body looked withered as one often sees in older people, but he was sprightly and had a twinkle to his eye.

Still feeling heat on my cheeks, I said, 'May I buy you a drink as an apology? Are you here alone?' Then I noticed his trousers; the upturn on the bottom of his right ankle was torn, I could see the material of his bright red socks through a hole in them. 'Oh, my goodness. Did I tear your trousers with my heel?' I knew I had gotten my right heel caught in something as I tried to extricate myself from him but had thought it to be the inner mesh of my own dress I had torn.

'Oh, it's nothing, my dear. This old thing was only good for the scrap pile anyway,' he said while indicating his dinner jacket. 'I should thank you for forcing me to throw it out.' He was being unfairly generous, much the same as I would hope to be in similar circumstances.

Alistair touched my arm. 'Will you be alright without me? I'm being called upon, I'm afraid.'

'Of course. You must go. I will see you again soon enough.' As Alistair moved away to make sure all the other guests were afforded a portion of his time, I hooked my arm through the older man's offered elbow and allowed him to escort me to the bar. 'I'm Patricia,' I said to introduce myself.

'Charlie,' he replied.

I grimaced at the name and he saw it. 'Sorry, I was... am married to a Charlie. We went our separate ways quite recently and I'm still smarting from it.'

'Goodness. It's so sad when two people cannot make their marriage work. Sue and I have been married for fifty-seven years. We were planning to do this for our sixtieth wedding anniversary, but we started to get nervous that one of us might not be here by then. So, we figured we might as well get on with it.'

'Fifty-seven years. That is a long time.'

'Yes,' he laughed. 'They get less for murder.' He laughed at his own joke and I smiled to play along.

Arriving at the bar, I swished my free hand at the array of drinks available. 'What can I get you?'

'A gin and tonic, I think.'

'A man after my own heart.' The barman heard him and nodded when I held up two fingers. He had been serving me for almost two months, so he knew how I liked mine now. 'And what can I get for your wife?'

Charlie raised his eyebrows in question. 'Wife? Oh no, dear. I'm not married.'

Confused, I said, 'But you were just telling me about Sue and that you have been married for fifty-seven years.'

'Was I?' He looked confused and was staring into the distance. My heart skipped as I worried that the lovely man might be suffering from dementia.

Just then a younger man appeared right behind him. 'Father, I wondered where you had got to. You know you are supposed to stay in one spot when I leave you.' He locked eyes with me. 'I hope he hasn't been any bother.'

'Not at all,' I assured Charlie's son with a smile. 'I bumped into him. I offered to buy him a drink as my apology.' The man looked at least my age, but probably a little older which made him about the right age to be Charlie's son. Like everyone else, he was wearing a dinner jacket though his was a dark navy blue and looked to be hand cut. It fit him very well and though he was going a little doughy, like most middle-aged men, he gave off a sense of intelligent capability. 'Can I get you something as well?' I asked.

The man saw the gin and tonic arrive in front of his father and swooped on it. 'You know you cannot drink on your medication, Father.' He switched his gaze to look at me as he lifted the drink. 'I'll have this one.' Then turned his attention to the barman standing expectantly right in front of him. 'An orange juice for my father, please.'

Embarrassed yet again, I felt my cheeks glowing as I said, 'I'm sorry. I didn't know.'

The man, who hadn't bothered to introduce himself gave me a weary look. 'You weren't to know. He saw the posters for this event and wanted to enter the draw. I indulged him but I never thought he would win a ticket. Now here we are, but he won't remember it even if we stay.'

I couldn't think of anything to say. I didn't need to defend myself, the man wasn't attacking me, he just seemed sad about his father. He downed the gin and tonic I bought for his father in one swift hit then spun his father's bar stool around. 'Come along, Father. We need to get to our seats.'

'But I haven't finished my drink yet,' Charlie protested. His son led him away, the old, confused man letting himself be ordered about as if accepting that it was the best thing for him. I hung my head, sad that I could do nothing positive to make things better for the nice man I just met. Senility, dementia, they were such cruel companions. I grabbed my own gin and tonic from the bar and knocked it back in an angry gesture at the planet for allowing such afflictions to exist.

The gin passed through me with a shudder, partly from the cold and partly from the hard hit of alcohol and I stamped my foot twice as I recovered from it. Life was unfair, that was something we all have to accept. That was what I told myself as I stared into nothing and thought about the universe. It was a good thing that my ugly train of thought was interrupted by the call to take our seats.

The Show Can't Go On

It was probably a blessing that the show had to get started on time. Ushers from the television crew encouraged people to take their seats fifteen minutes before the show was due to begin airing and all the dancers left just before that. The show brought its own musicians along, displacing the ship's band and they were set up near the entrance to allow enough room for the dancefloor in the centre of the restaurant. The judges' panel was at the far end and the spectators seating arranged on both long sides.

Alistair and I, along with several other VIP guests, were seated not far from the judges with an enviable view from the far end of the dance floor. I spotted Barbie when she came in, waving to her as she took her seat. Time ticked on and everyone got ready, the cameras were in place but sitting so close to the judges, I was among the first to get a sense that something was amiss. Irani was nowhere in sight and the show was due to start very soon. The cameras were swinging around and the producer, an Indian woman with a severe hairstyle, and severe glasses was looking agitated.

Excited television crew people with clipboards and headsets were rushing about and bumping into one another, hushed voices were nevertheless insistent about something. I watched the clock tick down and all the cameras get into position. Everything was ready to go, and I could see the dancers nervously lining up through the doors at the bottom of the dance floor.

Just as the producer woman, who looked to be in charge, came to the judges table with a worried expression, the smiling show host appeared from between the dancers at the far end of the ballroom. He had a sheen of sweat on his forehead, I could see it even across the length of the dancefloor. A microphone was thrust into his hand, two cameras swung around on their boom arms to zoom on his face, and a man counted him in.

There was hushed silence as he reached three, switched to using his fingers, counted down to one, and pointed to him. The host was on air. 'Good evening, ladies and gentlemen and welcome to this special edition of *Stars that Dance* filmed live on board the Aurelia, prized jewel of Purple Star Lines. But now, without further ado, I give you our dancers!' As he roared the final word, the dancers began sweeping onto the dance floor and music filled the room.

The spectacle began and I found myself instantly absorbed by it. A voiceover announcer talked while the dancers twirled and spun in a choreographed routine. Each couple was introduced including Dayita and her partner, apparently an Olympic star, as the announcer explained that she was injured and would not be taking part this week. Her partner waved gamely as a camera swung to him, but his smile looked forced and his dance partner was nowhere to be seen, the seat next to him obviously empty.

As the first routine finished, the dancers all swept back out through the curtains at the far end of the dancefloor and quiet descended again. Irani Patel was a consummate show host, completely in control of his environment and very much at home in front of the camera. He talked for a couple of minutes, filling in while the dancers reset themselves. Then it was time for the individual couples to show what they could do for the judges and the voters at home.

First up was Taginda Gill, the rather unpleasant woman from earlier, who I now discovered was a star of several television programs. Her dancer, Rajesh, was lithe and graceful next to the shorter and slightly plump woman, but as they performed a quick step I thought she did very well. The judges though were harsh with her, pointing out technical deficiencies and a lack of style. Her marks from the panel were low too though I got the impression they were about par for her and the home vote would see her through.

With a final bow and wave, Taginda and Rajesh were finished, and the next dancers were announced. The next dancers were Amya and Henri. They were to perform a Viennese waltz. The music started up again and they swept on to the floor, Irani Patel stepped back into the shadows as the cameras turned their attention to the dancers.

When they finished a few minutes later, the same process of the host speaking and the dancers being judged took place. This time though, as they left the ballroom through the curtain at the bottom, Irani Patel said, 'We're going for a short break where you can hear from our sponsors. Don't go anywhere. There'll be more live action in just a moment as Vihaan and Arabella perform a Charleston.' The moment the cameraman showed he was clear, the smile dropped and Irani's instantly looked troubled. I was curious about it but for no good reason. I took my leave to powder my nose and made my way around the back of the seats down the long side of the dancefloor.

The toilets for the top deck restaurant were immediately outside the entrance but there was already a queue for the ladies. I didn't feel like waiting and my suite really wasn't very far away; I could go there instead. I didn't get there though; a scream stopped me short. It came from inside the ladies' toilet and everyone heard it.

The ladies inside were now trying to get out and the ladies outside were trying to see in, their natural curiosity demanding they identify what was causing the fuss. The inevitable logjam burst as the women inside barged through.

'What's going on?' asked one of a pair of security guards rushing to the scene in response to the screams.

Running by him, a woman in a cocktail dress shouted, 'There's so much blood!' before disappearing in the crowd moving away from the toilet.

The two security guards exchanged a glance. Then, as the toilet emptied, they went in. I followed, my own curiosity forcing me to investigate. Instantly I could see what the ladies had reacted to; a pool of blood was spreading out from under the door of the final stall.

The lead man stepped cautiously up to the door and knocked. 'Madam? Madam, are you alright in there?' When no answer came back, he reached into a pocket to produce a fold out multi-tool. 'I'm going to open it,' he announced, his face betraying how unhappy he was about performing the task.

Just as he approached the door, more white uniforms spilled into the room including Alistair who put a hand on my shoulder. 'You should not be in here, Patricia.' He was trying to protect me rather than telling me to go, but it was too late to leave now as the stall door popped open with a click and there, for all to see, was Dayita with a large knife sticking out of her chest.

She was fully clothed and still wearing the same figure-hugging, black, sequinned outfit from earlier. She was clearly dead though, her lifeless eyes staring disbelievingly at the knife's handle.

Then I noticed the calling card. The same little white card with the signature and the brush stroke was impaled by the knife and stuck to her chest.

A Mystery to Solve

Alistair huffed out a breath as he stared at the dead woman before us. Then he started giving orders. 'Lieutenant Baker secure this area. No one comes in here unless they are crew and have a task to perform. Schneider, I want you to fetch Dr Kim, he needs to record time of death, deal with the body and possibly perform an autopsy.' If anything, his voice was sad.

'Do you want me to fetch Commander Yusef?' asked Baker, referring to the new deputy captain. His hand paused over the button on his radio while he waited for the captain's response.

Alistair shook his head. 'No. I will inform him of the incident, but I will deal with this myself.' Then he turned to me. 'Patricia, I'm afraid I will be tied up for the rest of the evening. I think it's safe to assume that the show tonight will now be cancelled.' As he said that though, we all heard the music start up once more and Irani Patel's voice echoing in the background as he announced two more dancers.

'Maybe they don't know,' I said in answer to the unvoiced question.

'They'll find out soon enough.' Alistair's face was grim. 'I will have to tell them. We cannot let the show continue; everyone involved in it is a murder suspect.'

With me hot on his heels, he left the plush white marble of the ladies' top deck toilet on his way back to the ballroom. I slid to a stop though as my eye caught something glinting on the tile. As I bent to get a closer look, Lieutenant Baker saw me. 'What have you got there, Mrs Fisher?'

I knew what it was before I picked it up; it was a blue opal. A very rare blue opal I had very recently seen attached to Irani Patel's cufflink. I doubted there were more of them on board. I explained what it was to Lieutenant Baker as he placed it into an evidence bag.

'I will need to show this to the captain,' he said, straightening up and offering his hand to get me back on my feet.

'We shouldn't jump to any conclusions.'

'I promise that I won't, Mrs Fisher. Others might though. If this is his, then why is it in the ladies' toilet? He would have no reason to come in here by himself.' I had no answer to his question, it felt a little damning, and why was there a calling card stuck to the dead woman?

Baker left another man in charge of the scene and hurried off to find Alistair. As he did, I headed back to my seat, curious to see what would happen now. As I walked quickly around the back of the temporary raised seating erected for the event, a voice called, 'Hey.'

I turned and could see someone hiding in the shadows at the edge of the ballroom. It was a man and I thought it might be Taginda's dance partner, Rajesh, just from the little bit of costume I could see. He was behind a large plant though, peering through the fronds at me, gesturing for me to come closer. There was no one else around to see us; everyone in the room was on the other side of the raised seating we were now behind. 'Can I help you?' I asked cautiously. A woman had just been murdered and there was a man hiding in a plant now. I wasn't getting too close just in case.

He waved frantically for me to come closer, then ducked behind the plant and I lost him from sight. Nervously, I moved into the shadows whereupon my foot crunched on something. I moved my foot and looked down.

As I moved my foot back, I saw what I had stood on. It was a pregnancy test; the type the hopeful mother pees on. When I picked it up, I could clearly see that it had been used and clearly read pregnant next to two thick black lines. The man I still hadn't identified, said, 'Get that to the captain,' and then was gone, slipping away among the darkness and ornate plants at the edge of the restaurant. This had to mean something, but I was going to have to find out who the man was first and what his connection might be to anyone. What was he trying to tell me? That Dayita was pregnant? That someone else was pregnant? It was too cryptic for me to have the faintest idea what it might mean yet.

Tapping the test against my fingernails as I thought, the music once again wound down as the dance I couldn't see came to an end with rapturous applause. It was replaced after almost a minute by the sound of Irani Patel's voice as he too congratulated the couple on their performance and launched into an anecdote about once dancing the waltz for a film he made many years ago.

I crept back toward my seat to get a view of what was happening. Surely, the host was about to announce that the show's live performance had to be terminated and then provide a reason of some kind for it. He didn't though; the couple, having just finished the energetic dance, were breathing heavily and standing in front of the judges' panel waiting for feedback.

Alistair was on the far side of the room and visibly arguing with the severe-looking producer woman running the show. I couldn't get to them because I would have to walk behind the judges to do so, but it looked like he was arguing for the show to be stopped and meeting with determined refusal.

I wasn't doing any good here and I had no further interest in the show. A woman had been murdered and there was a mystery to solve. Whether

Alistair liked it or not, I was going to interfere and the first thing I needed to do was speak with Dr Kim. He was just arriving at the ladies' toilet when I got back outside. The white uniforms of the ship's security team had cordoned off the area and stewards were directing ladies to the next nearest set of toilets in the upper deck gymnasium.

'Dr Kim,' I called to get his attention, raising my hand when he looked up to see who it was. 'Dr Kim, before you go in there.'

He paused near the door to wait for me. 'Good evening, Mrs Fisher. Another terrible incident awaits me.' He looked glum.

'Yes. I'm sure this is not the best element of your job. There's something you need to check on the victim though.'

'Oh. What's that?'

'She might be pregnant.' I showed him the pregnancy test. 'One of the male dancers left this for me to find. I don't know why, but it might have something to do with why she was killed.' Dr Kim nodded his understanding and went inside. Left in the passageway, I decided it was time to get my butler. Jermaine was great to have around and good for bouncing ideas off. I hurried to my suite, passing the upper deck gymnasium and the queue of ladies lined up to use the facilities within. Around the corner, I bumped into Charlie, the delightful old man with the dodgy memory.

I stopped to check on him. 'Charlie, are you alright? I thought you were watching the show with your son.' He had dust on his suit and a cobweb, both of which I tried to brush off without him noticing I was doing it as I linked my arm with his again.

He looked embarrassed to be caught wandering the passageways alone. 'Oh, I, ah. Yes, I went to the gents but then took a wrong turn somewhere and ended up here. Do you know how to get back to the ballroom?'

I really wanted to get into my suite so I could use the bathroom myself, but the sweet old man had to take priority. 'I'll see you get back safely, shall I?' Then arm in arm, I went back to the ballroom yet again. 'Do you know where you are sitting?' I asked him, hoping he would be able to give me an answer this time.

He looked about though, tapping his top lip with his fingernails. 'Just over there, I think. I don't see my son though.' I couldn't see him either, but, just like last time, he found us.

'Father, there you are.' His son looked relieved again. 'I swear I turned my back for a second and he was gone. I don't know how he moves so fast. Thank you for returning him.'

I shot him a smile. 'That's quite alright. He's very sweet.' The son thanked me once again, doing a good job of looking after his father in tough circumstances. I watched them make their way back to their seats just as Irani flamboyantly announced the next dancers. As the music started, I ducked back out and ran straight into Barbie.

'Patty, what's with all the security around the ladies' toilet? I asked the guys there, but they wouldn't tell me anything.'

I pulled her to one side, hooking her arm. 'I'll tell you on the way.'

'On the way where?'

'To get Jermaine. We have a mystery to solve.'

Clues

'Madam, you have a spot of paint on you.' Jermaine emerged from his adjoining cabin two seconds after Barbie and I came through the front door to my suite. Somehow he was always ready and dressed and expecting me. Of course, I now had a tiny canine alert system to tell him I was home. Anna had leapt from her position asleep on the couch the moment the door started to open. Barking her indignation at being disturbed, she calmed when she saw it was me. By then, of course Jermaine was through the kitchen and into my living space. He spotted the paint instantly.

I looked down at myself. 'Where?'

Barbie was staring too and had there been anyone watching it would have looked as if the three of us were examining my boobs. 'Just here, madam.' He pointed to himself to indicate where I should look. 'Perhaps looking in the mirror will help.'

I moved a few feet to the full-length mirror by the entrance lobby. There was indeed a blob of paint on my dress. It was right under my left breast and thus impossible for me to see without a mirror. The paint was a bright yellow but only the size of a fingertip. 'It's dry,' I said as I scratched at it. 'It wasn't there when I put it on.'

'Where did you find wet paint?' asked Barbie.

'I have no idea,' I said with a grumpy sigh. The dress, which had not been cheap, was ruined most likely. I doubted the mark would come out. I tried licking a finger and rubbing it. 'It's not water-soluble either.'

Jermaine stood back and fell into his relaxed butler's pose where he waited for instruction. 'I wasn't expecting you back so soon, madam. Was the show not to your liking?'

Barbie answered him, 'There's been a murder.'

His eyes and nostrils flared in surprise. 'Another one?'

'They are getting to be a habit,' I conceded. 'I'm going to change.' With a final tut at my ruined dress, I began undoing the zip at the side and stomped across the carpet to my bedroom. I could hear Barbie filling Jermaine in on the little we already knew as I stripped off my dress and looked in my wardrobe for something else. Would I go back to the ballroom? It still surprised me that the show hadn't been interrupted but I might need to go back in, so I selected another ball gown from the rack, thankful that I had more than one that fitted me.

Then, I spotted it, my heart freezing and a cold shudder zipping up my spine as I spun around to stare.

On my nightstand was a little white calling card. 'Jermaine!' I shouted, my legs feeling weak from shock. I could hear feet running, my butler ditching decorum for speed as he raced to see what urgent need I had.

He and Barbie burst into my bedroom seconds later, Jermaine instantly stopping and turning about. 'Madam, you need a gown.'

Oops. In my shock, it hadn't registered that all I had on was my knickers; the ball gown didn't allow for a bra to be worn underneath. Barbie grabbed a robe from the en suite bathroom. 'Patty, what is it? What made you shout? I half expected to find another body in here.'

I pointed to the nightstand. 'That's the same calling card the murdered girl had impaled onto her chest with a kitchen knife.'

Barbie gasped and Jermaine hung his head. 'Someone was in the suite and I didn't hear them,' he said, his voice full of shame.

I touched his arm, trying to impart that he couldn't protect the suite from all invaders. 'Have you been out?'

He lifted his head. 'Yes. I went to the crew gym. I was out for almost an hour indulging myself when I should have been protecting the suite.'

'Nonsense, Jermaine. You cannot be here every second of every day. I want to know what this is about though. Apparently, these cards have been popping up for weeks, exclusively in the top deck suites but nothing has ever been taken. We need to check now and see if we can find anything out of place or missing. Then we need to tell security, this could affect their investigation.'

'Very good, madam.' He about turned and went back into the suite's main living area where he began to check cupboards and cabinets. There were several expensive objects in the suite; oil paintings on the walls and other items such as vases in locked glass display cabinets.

'We should check the safe,' suggested Barbie. I quickly zipped up my dress and crouched to examine the calling card. I didn't touch it, and I didn't know what I was looking for, but it was evidence of something and that made it important. It confused me that the same card was impaled on the knife that killed Dayita. She had been on the ship for barely more than a day, but the calling cards started appearing long before that. Were the two connected or not?

'We should check the safe,' Barbie said again, breaking my concentration.

I stood up. 'Yes, we should. Let's do that now.'

We found Jermaine back out in the living area. He was over by the kitchen and looking through the drawers there. 'I cannot find anything out of place, madam. Whoever was in here to leave that card, doesn't seem to have taken anything.'

'It's so strange,' I muttered. Anna pawed at my foot. She followed me around only when she wanted something and seemed quite independent the rest of the time. Usually, when she made a point of getting my attention, she wanted a biscuit. It was probably the case this time, but as I glanced down at her, I caught sight of something. Staring down at the carpet, I called for my butler, 'Jermaine, can you look at something over here please?'

Moving at his glacial butler's pace once more, he crossed the room. Next to me, Barbie had followed my gaze, but she couldn't see what I was seeing. 'Is Anna okay?' she asked, wondering if I was concerned about my dog.

I pointed to the carpet. 'Can you see the four indentations?' I moved my finger around to show them all four. 'And the dust over there?' I pointed to a line of dust.

'I'll have that cleared up in a jiffy, madam.'

'No, Jermaine. This is a clue. I think. I saw the same marks and line of dust on the carpet in Irani Patel's room earlier. When Barbie and I came past his room earlier, he was arguing with Deepa Bhukari about the card he found in his room, but I noticed on the floor by his feet, four odd little indentations in a perfect rectangle. See how it looks like something heavy was here and now it isn't?'

Barbie and Jermaine both nodded. That was what it looked like. In the carpet near my safe were four small indentations like the feet of a table would leave behind if it sat in the same spot for a time and was then moved.

'What could have made it?' asked Barbie.

It was a question that had me stumped and what the line of dust meant I had no idea. 'Can you take some photographs with your phone?' I asked her before turning to Jermaine. 'Do we have a tape measure somewhere? I want to compare this to the one in Mr Patel's room.'

'Of course, madam.'

While Jermaine fetched a measure and Barbie clicked pictures with her phone, I opened the safe. It was hidden behind a large oil painting that hinged out from one side. I didn't have much in there because I am a woman of limited means. It was a point I should probably start worrying about as I have no income once I return home to England in a few more weeks, but I did have a reserve of cash I was hoarding to get me through the first few months. The cash came as an insurance payout from recovering the sapphire, but I would need it to set myself up in a new home, buy new furniture, organise my life and all the other things that follow a separation. I felt a minor flutter of worry that the safe might be empty when I opened the door, but it wasn't. The cash, my passport and a few other items were just as they had been last time I looked.

'What is this person's motive?' I asked myself. When Barbie looked at me, I started talking. 'They break in to the suites on the top deck where most of the guests are very rich people but they don't take anything. They risk being caught each time they enter someone else's cabin, but they have been doing it for weeks. They even leave a calling card as if bragging that they cannot be caught.'

'What about the murder?' Barbie asked. 'Do you think maybe Dayita disturbed the person and he or she killed her to protect their identity?'

I shrugged. 'If she disturbed someone in her room, surely she would have been killed in her room. Also, the celebrities are all staying in suites, but I don't think the professional dancers are. If this calling card criminal only breaks in to suites, then he couldn't have bumped into Dayita.'

'Unless she was in someone else's suite,' said Jermaine.

That put a new spin on things. 'If she was involved with one of the celebrities then that could easily be the case.' I thought about that for a second. 'Who would it be? Taginda said she was sleeping with Rajesh, Taginda's dance partner, but also said he was gay though he instantly denied it.'

Barbie looked at Jermaine. 'You've got a good nose for this. If you met Rajesh would you be able to tell if he is gay or not.'

'That depends,' my tall butler replied. 'If he is still hiding it, it is far harder to know to any degree of accuracy.'

I walked across to the desk and the computer there. 'The question really, is whether Dayita was also sleeping with one of the celebrities and if so which one? Can you find out which cabin she was staying in. There may be clues there and I want to check that the four indentations don't appear in her room.'

As Jermaine slid in front of the computer, I continued to think about what I had seen at the show. 'Barbie, did you notice how late Irani Patel was to arrive this evening?'

'Yeah. The show almost started without him.' We locked eyes, both thinking the same thing at the same time. 'Do you think she could have been involved with him? Was she in his suite and got disturbed by the calling card criminal there?'

I thought about it but shook my head. 'It doesn't fit. I mean, she might have been involved with him, but I saw her alive after the calling card was found in his suite and I raise the point again about killing her in the suite. If she walked in on the calling card person, she would get killed there, not taken to a ladies toilet. She had to have been killed in the toilet. Plus...'

Barbie waited for me to finish my sentence, then, when I didn't, she prompted me, 'Plus...' she drawled.

'Plus I found a gem from one of his cufflinks in the ladies toilet.'

She threw her arms in the air. 'Well, that's it then. Nothing else to it. No mystery to solve.' I thought about it, but something didn't feel right. She persisted though. 'Think about it. All the dancers were lined up to dance so none of them could have killed Dayita. The judges were in their seats, but the host was missing, and no one seemed to know where he was. And he looked sweaty like he had been doing something strenuous,' Barbie added. Then she saw my expression. 'You don't look convinced.'

'I'm not,' I admitted. 'There's something here that doesn't fit. Right now, I want to say that it could be anyone. Or, more accurately, it could be lots of people. He has to be on the list of suspects though.' Then there was the pregnancy test. I told them both about that and what it could mean.

Barbie felt that it reinforced her willingness to convict Irani Patel though. 'If Dayita was pregnant and having an affair with Irani, then he killed her to escape the scandal.'

Facts were stacking up against the host, that was for sure. I grabbed my phone. 'We are going to need reinforcements.'

Reinforcements

Rick and Akamu had been playing blackjack in one of the onboard casinos. There were three of them on different decks, but they could only open in certain territories. Some countries didn't allow gambling so when the Aurelia was in their waters, the casinos were closed. Out at sea though, they were open, and the chaps were having a flutter.

'Hi, Patricia. Got a new murder for us to solve?' asked Rick as he answered the phone. He was being flippant but had hit the truth, nevertheless.

'I do actually. Are you guys sober?'

'I'm nursing a bourbon and ice but yeah, we're sober. Mostly. I lose badly enough without trying to play cards drunk,' he laughed. 'Has there really been a murder?'

'I'm afraid so. Can you come to my suite?'

That conversation was half an hour old now and they were just coming through the door. I had Anna tucked under my right arm because she was going nuts with all the intruders she needed to kill. The captain and three members of his security team including Lieutenant Baker were already with us. I placed the call to Alistair after I spoke with Rick, told him about the calling card in my bedroom and he appeared less than five minutes later. Now he had chaps in my bedroom dusting for prints.

When I showed Alistair the four indentations in my carpet and the line of dust, he knelt to examine it. 'And you say you saw the same marks on the carpet in Mr Patel's suite?'

'I'm fairly sure. I didn't get to go into his suite though, so I was looking at it from several yards away.'

'I can fix that.' Alistair stood up and removed a keycard from his right breast pocket. 'Universal keycard,' he said to tell me what it was. 'Let's have a look at his suite.' Leaving just the two security guys in my bedroom dusting for prints, the rest of us traipsed out of my cabin, along the passageway and into Mr Patel's suite next door.

Sure enough, on the floor in front of the safe were four small indentations and a line of dust just beyond them.

Seven of us stared at the little dents in the carpet. 'They look the same size and spacing to me,' I observed.

Jermaine chose that moment to crouch, the tape measure appearing in his hand. 'They are exactly the same, madam,' he concluded almost immediately.

'But what does that tell us?' asked Baker, scratching his head.

Alistair folded his arms and cupped his chin. 'That whoever is leaving the calling cards is doing something when they are in the cabin. They break in, they perform a task which somehow creates four dents in the carpet and a line of dust. Then they leave a calling card and go. It is also worth noting that they gain entry without needing to force their way in, so they have a universal card in their possession or some other way of getting in.'

'What does this have to do with the dead girl and anyone from the Indian TV show? asked Akamu.

We all looked at each other, each of us equally perplexed. The sound of running feet went by outside the suite's door. Then the sound of a conversation in the passageway outside. It sounded like it was coming from my suite and the footsteps came running back a few seconds later followed by a frantic knocking on the door.

Baker, being the nearest, opened it. Young Lieutenant Pippin was outside and he looked flushed with excitement. He spotted the captain and cracked out a swift salute. 'Sir, the show is ending. The producer lady in charge is looking for you to say a few words for the camera.'

Alistair twitched his mouth in aggravation. 'I certainly have a few words to say to her. And a few awkward questions to pose to Mr Patel. In the meantime, Lieutenant Baker, please continue with the investigation. Use whatever resources you need. I will find you again shortly at the after party, yes?' Then he was gone, following Pippin back to the ballroom with a tight-lipped smile in my direction as he left.

There was no reason to stay in Irani Patel's suite but every reason to visit Dayita's cabin. Jermaine had found it easily enough using the ship's central registry system. It was three decks down where an entire passageway had been emptied for the TV crew and dancers to occupy.

'What will you do now?' I asked Baker.

He frowned in thought. 'Despite the stack of evidence against Mr Patel, I need to start interviewing the cast and the crew of the TV show and we have to appeal for witnesses to come forward. We also have to break the news of the murder; I don't think any of the dancers or celebrities know yet.'

'Someone knows,' Rick commented grimly. 'Someone killed her.'

No one had a response. We started to move toward the door as Baker asked, 'What will you do, Mrs Fisher?'

'Well, you still have chaps in my suite so I think we will stay out until they are finished. I'm going to see if I can't work out who was sleeping with who. There seems to be at least one love triangle going on here and it has cost one life already.'

Outside in the passageway, we split up; Baker heading toward the ballroom to continue the investigation and the rest of us heading in the other direction. I still had Anna under my arm, and she was getting heavy. She was barely awake though, quite content to be carried around like a baby. We needed to walk to find Dayita's cabin so I figured I might as well walk her at the same time.

I stopped Rick and Akamu before I set off. 'Chaps, I have a task that will suit you.' I explained what I hoped they could do and what I hoped they would be able to discover and left them to it.

Then with Barbie and Jermaine, I set off for the elevators.

Smoking Gun

Dayita's cabin was on the seventeenth deck but all the way back toward the stern which meant even using elevators we had most of a kilometre to walk. Jermaine had a universal door card we *borrowed* from a cleaner a while ago and forgot quite deliberately to ever give back. It was surprising how often we were able to justify using it.

He swiped on the control pad and the little click and green light told us we were in. At my feet, Anna was pawing at the door to get inside. She had no idea what was on the other side of the door, of course, but her dog brain always wanted to be on the other side of a locked door. We got a shock when we pushed the door open though; inside, the cabin was turned upside down.

'Wow! Do you think they were burgled?' asked Barbie.

I cast my eyes around and could see jewellery and a purse. 'That depends on whether anything has been taken. It looks more like the room was tossed by someone looking for something. I can see cash over there by the bed.' I pointed.

'So what were they looking for?' asked Jermaine. 'That's a task for us to find out.'

I put my arms out to stop the others from moving. 'This is also part of a crime scene so we can't leave our fingerprints anywhere and need to make sure we don't move anything.'

Barbie sucked on her teeth. 'Should we be in here at all?'

I shook my head. 'Definitely not. However, we are now, so let's have a quick look around, touch as little as possible and get out again.' I tucked Anna under my arm again, fighting her as she wriggled to explore as well.

Then the three of us started picking through various pieces of the cabin. The cabins were being shared, two girls in one, two guys in another. I guess the TV show has a limited budget and cruise ships aren't the cheapest places on earth. The room was such a mess though, I struggled to work out whose items were whose. I couldn't even be sure which bed belonged to which girl.

I went into the bathroom and poked about in the trashcan there. Sure enough, I found the wrapper for a pregnancy test. 'Look at this, guys,' I said, using a piece of tissue from my pocket to pick it up.

Barbie stared at it. 'We still don't know if that is Dayita's or belonged to her roommate but I'd be willing to bet Dayita was pregnant.'

'That's certainly how it looks, but if that is why she was killed? Who is the father?'

'Madam?' called Jermaine to get my attention. 'I have carefully cleared as much of the floor as I can but can find no indentations. It may be that they were already rubbed out by traffic moving over them though,' he suggested.

I didn't think so though. 'According to the captain, the calling cards have only been found in the top deck suites. I can't see our mystery player leaving the top deck just to come down here.'

'But you said Dayita had one of the calling cards pinned to her with the knife,' Barbie pointed out. 'That sounds personal. Like they wanted everyone to know who killed her.'

'Murder would also be a big escalation from sneaking into rooms and not taking anything,' I countered. Neither Barbie nor Jermaine could argue with me. 'If the calling card criminal killed Dayita, then I don't know why.'

'Should we go?' asked Barbie.

I really wanted to explore. Somewhere in this room could be the answer to why a woman had lost her life this evening. It was part of a crime scene though and we were already contaminating it. 'Is everything as you found it?' I asked them both.

When they nodded, the three of us backed toward the door and left. As I closed the door, Jermaine shot his hand into the closing gap. 'One moment please, madam. I just spotted something. Barbie, may I borrow your phone?' Barbie handed it over, Jermaine taking it and turning on the torch function as he crept forward into the room again.

'What is it?' Barbie asked, ducking down to see where Jermaine might be heading.

'It might be nothing,' he replied. 'There is something glinting beneath the cabinet though.' Shining the torch into the gap beneath the wooden cabinet, he got onto his hands and knees to reach in. Then stood back up with something in his hand. When he turned around to show me what it was, I gasped. It was a smoking gun. Jermaine held a blue opal and its presence in Dayita's room placed Irani Patel in here, sealing the suggestion that he was involved with her and was almost certainly the father of her baby and her killer.

Stunned by the revelation, because in my head it still didn't fit, I started back toward the elevator. 'We have to get back to the ballroom.'

Accusations

Because the top deck restaurant had been converted into the ballroom for the live TV event, the after party, where the stars of the show finally got to relax for a bit, was being held in a function room on the nineteenth deck. Tucked into the prow of the ship, it had an excellent view in daylight, but panoramic windows ensured it gave a suitable backdrop even at night as a blanket of stars seemed to envelope the ship.

I couldn't remember what time the after party was due to start but it had to be soon after the show itself finished and that was happening right about now. The after party was by invitation only due to the number of people that would want to attend and the size of the venue. Fortunately, yet again, I was on the list.

I called Alistair to see where he was currently. 'Hello, Patricia,' his dulcet tone echoed in my ear when the call connected. 'Where are you, my dear?'

'I'm just on my way to you if you tell me where you are. Have the cast of the show been told about Dayita yet?'

Alistair made a huffing sound of annoyance. 'No. It is just about to happen though. The show's producer insisted they could wait until the live show ended, which it just did. They are gathering on the dancefloor, all the cast and supporting staff from the studio, that is. I think they plan to tell them only once the audience has left. People are starting to depart now. It's a real party atmosphere in here, but that's about to change.'

'Did the show go well?' I asked.

'Yes, without a hitch and, according to the producer, they have the highest ever viewership for any show ever shown in India. They seem rather proud of the record, but I doubt that will be what they remember tonight for.'

We reached the elevator. 'I have to go. I'll join you in a few minutes.'

Getting in the elevator, I found my nerves rising. I felt unsettled that we held the news about Irani Patel. He had been in Dayita's room, but did that mean he had killed her? By itself it provided very little by way of evidence.

We rode the elevator back up to the top deck and walked at a quick pace to get back to the ballroom. Passing the ladies toilet outside the ballroom, the white uniforms of the security team were still keeping everyone away while they dealt with what was inside and I wondered if they had removed Dayita yet. Dr Kim would need to examine her to determine for certain if she had been pregnant or not, but further testing, beyond that which he could perform on the ship, would be required to demonstrate the baby had been Irani Patel's.

Outside the ballroom doors, a team of cleaners and other crew were waiting impatiently to get in. They were being held at bay by yet more security as they explained the ballroom was not yet ready. I spotted Lieutenant Schneider and waved to him, thankful that I knew enough members of the security team to bypass the queue.

'Are you looking for the captain?' he asked as we slipped inside the ballroom.

Schneider started leading us to him before I said, 'Most definitely. I have news to share with him.'

Through the curtains at the entrance to the ballroom where the stars had all made their grand entrances, I could see the celebrities and the dancers together with the judges and a host of TV crew all gathered in a gaggle at the far end near the judges' panel.

The cameras were off, and people looked relaxed, but it was clear they were waiting for something. As I approached, the producer of the show started talking. She was a small woman; I could only see her because she was standing on the stage at the far end. She had thick round glasses which distorted her eyes and hair pulled back into a bun. The clipboard I saw her with earlier was still in her right hand as she waved everyone into silence.

'Everyone, everyone, thank you. Thank you. Tonight, as you know, we broke the record for the highest ever audience in the history of Indian television.' A cheer ripped through the small crowd and she waved them to quiet again. 'I have other news though. Terrible news,' she added, her tone softening and her smile fading. 'I only learned of this recently and by then it was too late to stop the show, but I am burdened with giving the terrible news that Dayita was found dead earlier this evening.'

There was a sharp intake of breath from more than half the people present mixed with cries of shock and gasps of surprise.

'There is more,' the short woman explained, getting the crowd's attention once more. 'Her death was no accident. It would appear that Dayita was murdered.'

'She was murdered?' the shout came from Taginda near the front of the gathering.

'Yes.' This time it was Alistair that spoke. He stepped up next to the producer, taking over proceedings. 'At this time, we are still gathering evidence but it is clear that her death was not an accident. It will be necessary to interview each of you about your relationship and dealings with Dayita and about your movements immediately before the show started.' He let that information settle in for a moment.

Before he could speak again though, the producer added her thoughts, 'I am sure you will all join me in keeping Dayita and her family in your thoughts at this terrible time. The after party is still taking place and I am certain you will all honour her commitment to this show by attending. The show must go on.'

The crowd of stars and television crew were all talking over one another. No one was moving away though or making any attempt to get anywhere. Many looked unaffected by it but Taginda was holding her head in her hands and she looked sick.

I went around them all to get to Alistair. Before I got there a fight broke out.

'Say that again!' raged a petite woman, one of the professional dancers most likely. 'Say that again for everyone to hear!' She had hold of Taginda and was trying to grab her hair. The heavier woman was fighting her off and looked likely to send the smaller woman flying if she got a chance but other cast members stepped in to haul them apart before anyone could draw blood.

Irani positioned himself between the two women. 'What on earth is this about, Arabella? This is not the time to be attacking one another.'

'You didn't hear what she said,' Jasmin sobbed, tears running down her face now.

Rajesh, Taginda's dance partner, had hold of her shoulders having rushed in to help separate the women. 'Why, what did she say,' he spun Taginda around to face him. 'What did you say?'

Taginda said nothing but Jasmin was only too happy to fill in the blank. 'She was worried what impact Dayita's death might have on her votes.'

Everyone in the room looked at the plump TV star. Rajesh took his hands off her shoulders and backed away a pace.

'It's important for everyone,' protested Taginda. 'If they take the show off the air, we all lose.'

'My life, Taginda.' Rajesh's face was a mask of horror. 'I knew you were ambitious, but this is too much. You will have to find a new partner; I'm not dancing with you anymore. Dayita was my friend.'

'I thought she was your girlfriend,' Taginda snapped at him, her hands forming balled fists on her hips. 'Isn't that the lie you have been telling everyone? You're gay, Rajesh. You should just admit it and get on with your life.' Rajesh looked horrified at the attention he was now getting. He was rescued, but in a surprising way when a new voice joined the argument.

'I think we are all missing the point,' it was a man's voice, though he was hidden from view behind a press of other people. As they all turned to look at him, they also parted to reveal an older Indian gentleman. He was sitting in a chair, looking relaxed but also angry. His attention was focused on Irani Patel, the show's famous host. Now that everyone was looking at him, the man continued. 'Regardless of Rajesh's sexuality, though given how recently our country revoked the law making homosexuality illegal, I am not surprised he wishes to keep it secret, he isn't Dayita's killer.'

'You sound certain,' I said, speaking openly for the first time.

The man pierced me with his gaze. I thought he wanted to ask me to identify myself, but he decided that he didn't care or would find out later.

'It is obvious. Rajesh was just as surprised and horrified as the rest of us upon hearing the terrible news, but if he is gay, then he was using Dayita to hide his secret and has plenty to lose from her death.'

'Unless she threatened to out him,' snapped Taginda.

The man shook his head as he stood up. 'You all know me. You know my skills.'

'I don't,' I pointed out.

He carried on without acknowledging my comment. 'There is one among us who has a secret they would rather keep under wraps. Rajesh may have been having a fake relationship with Dayita...'

'It wasn't fake,' Rajesh protested, but no one was buying his story any longer.

The man continued despite the interruption. 'But another man was very much involved with Dayita.' He paused dramatically and gazed around to make sure he held everyone's attention. 'Isn't that right, Irani?'

There were several sharp intakes of breath as all eyes now swung to stare at the show host. His jaw fell open in surprise, but Taginda was nodding her head. 'I knew it. He's completely compromised his position. He'll have to go now.'

'Go where?' he asked.

'Just go,' replied Taginda with a sneeringly fake smile. 'Give up your position as host and let someone younger and better take over.'

Irani looked like he wanted to argue but his attention was drawn back to the taller man who had more to say. 'I saw you, Irani,' the man announced. 'I saw you more than once coming out of her cabin. Where were you right before the show started, Irani? Is that when you murdered her? Was she going to reveal your relationship?'

'Who is he?' I whispered to the person next to me, another one of the show's dancers.

He kept his eyes pointing directly ahead, unable to sway from the unfolding drama, but leaned his head in my direction as he answered, 'Devrani Bharma. He's famous as a TV detective but he was a police chief solving the crimes before he wrote the books that propelled him to stardom. Then they cast him in the lead role to play his own fictional detective based on his own life. On the show he always solves the crimes like this. His character watches and observes and always has the answer at the end.'

'Wow,' I murmured. It was quite the background.

He moved in close to Irani now, the crowd watching as he towered over the smaller man. 'Would you like to confess and save everyone a lot of trouble?'

The dancer next to me whispered, 'His character always says that. Then he says, "Take him downtown." And hands him over to one of the uniforms.'

Devrani Bharma motioned to the nearest uniform, Lieutenant Baker, and said, 'Take him downtown.' It was a dismissive statement intended to make him look superior and the criminal look guilty.

Lieutenant Baker looked unsure about what he was supposed to do at this point. He glanced at Irani Patel and then at Devrani Bharma and then at the captain, who was watching with amusement at his subordinate's confusion.

Alistair took it upon himself to get involved at this point. Stepping forward he said, 'Perhaps we ought to have a chat about your movements, Mr Patel. Can you show me the calling card you refused to hand over to my staff earlier?'

'Of course.' Irani Patel reached into his jacket, looking for the card in an inside pocket. He looked calm and confident but only for a second. It was instantly clear that he hadn't found it and was then checking the pocket on the other side of his jacket. Then he was patting all his pockets and starting to look worried.

'Where is it, Irani?' asked Devrani Bharma, adding unwelcome pressure. The show host looked bewildered. The attention of the room was all focused on him and I thought he was going to panic, but he took a deep breath and forced himself to face down his accuser. 'I must have put it down somewhere. I have done nothing wrong and I certainly didn't murder Dayita; my presence in her room is not suspicious. I visit many of the people involved in the show.'

'You've never visited me,' argued Taginda.

'Nor me,' claimed another and then another as most of the cast chipped in that his statement was false.

'Where were you immediately before the show?' Devrani asked.

Irani looked about with panicked eyes, his forced confidence gone again. He was the centre of attention which you might think he was used to, but he had the look of someone that wanted to bolt for the door. Lieutenant Schneider moved to cover the exit just in case but as Irani searched for a reply, it was his wife that spoke up.

'He was with me,' she said, her quiet voice almost inaudible even in the silent room. Heads turned to look her way and a pair of dancers standing together moved to one side to reveal the small woman. Her head was bowed, and she was staring at the deck.

Grasping the lifeline, Irani said, 'Yes. I was with my wife.'

'What were you doing?' asked Devrani, his expression making it clear he didn't believe either one of them. 'You were sweating profusely when you started the show. What was it that caused such strenuous exertion, Irani?'

Irani blinked, still struggling to find words and looking guiltier by the second.

'We were having sex,' his wife said quietly, her eyes still focused on the deck.

Irani, as if sensing that he now truly had an alibi, crossed the room to take his wife's hand. 'You see?' he asked the room while wrapping his wife into a hug. 'I shouldn't have to answer such questions. Your prying has forced my wife to reveal personal information you have no right to know. We are an affectionate couple with an active sex life. She came to me right before the show and I lost track of time. Isn't that right, darling?'

The small Indian woman nodded her head. She appeared ashamed, though she had provided her husband with a credible alibi. I still had the opal from his cufflinks which placed him in Dayita's room at some point between the champagne reception and the start of the show and had given over the opal from the toilet floor. The opal in her cabin didn't make him guilty of murdering her, but I had to question why he was going there if it were not to continue an illicit affair. The opal in the toilet just made him look guilty. That he had been going to her cabin was not in question though, he had admitted as much himself but dismissed it as insignificant. I wasn't sure that it was, but with the alibi his wife provided, it was now down to us to prove his guilt. I didn't think it would take long.

Devrani Bharma appeared to have no further questions but had turned his attention away from Irani and was now conversing with Alistair.

The producer woman, with her severe hair and glasses clapped her hands to get everyone's attention. 'I'm sorry,' she called out to make sure everyone was listening. 'We still have the show's after party to film. Despite this tragedy, the show must go on.' It wasn't the first time she had made that statement. 'We are the highest rated show in Indian television history; we have to capitalise on that, and the cameras are waiting for us. If you truly feel that you cannot continue with the show tonight, please see me afterwards, otherwise, please all now start moving to the room prepared for us on deck nineteen.'

'What about him?' Yet again it was Taginda that was causing a commotion. 'Did he kill Dayita or not? Shouldn't we lock him up or something?'

Irani managed to look indignant. 'You heard my wife. I was with her when Dayita was killed.'

The producer also had an argument. 'Taginda we need the host of the show. How can we film the after party without the host there?'

'I can host it,' she replied with a smile. 'I'm the most popular, the viewers would love it.' Several sets of eyebrows went up at her brazenness though I don't think she noticed or cared.

Before anyone else could respond, Alistair stepped onto the stage next to the producer lady. 'Ladies and gentlemen, as the captain, I am ultimately responsible for security on board this ship. There has been a murder and I intend to find the culprit. My security team will require each of you to answer some questions tonight and will be calling each of you forward over the next few hours.'

'They won't interrupt the after party show, will they?' asked the producer, looking concerned.

Alistair offered her a sympathetic smile. 'We will do what we can to be unobtrusive, but my investigation will not be impeded. I hope we can work together on this.' He was making it clear that he was in charge and the smaller woman, though she looked unhappy about it, bit her lip and offered no argument.

As he moved away from her, crossing the room to speak with Devrani again, she started herding the stars and dancers toward the door at the far end of the ballroom. They would move to the location for the after party one deck down, but they were unlikely to do it peacefully. I could hear bickering before they reached the doors and I wondered what misadventure this evening might yet bring.

A Challenge

As the stars of the show left the room, I waited for Alistair. He was deep in conversation with Devrani Bharma, the true-life detective turned television star. Waiting patiently for instruction were several of the captain's lieutenants. I chose to wait also, keeping a polite distance, but with Barbie and Jermaine also waiting for me, I have to admit that I didn't wait very long.

'Alistair,' I called to interrupt him. The two men were discussing the case in hushed tones, the nature of the conversation clear even though I couldn't hear exactly what they were saying. I felt a little shut out. Alistair didn't respond immediately. He glanced my way, then went back to speaking with Devrani. It was clear he was trying to conclude their discussion so he could give me his attention, so again I waited. A few seconds later, the two men both turned my way.

Alistair offered me a broad smile as he guided his new companion toward me. 'Patricia, allow me to introduce Devrani Bharma. Devrani is…'

'A famous television detective with a real-life background in police work,' I finished his sentence, surprising him that I already knew the man's identity. I shook Devrani's hand. 'I must say it is an impressive story. Will you be lending your talent to our efforts tonight?'

His brow creased in confusion. 'Our efforts?'

Alistair jumped in. 'Aha, yes, Mrs Fisher is something of an amateur sleuth. She has provided the solution to several mysteries in her short time on board.'

Devrani let my hand go. 'Yes, well, I think it prudent that we limit the number of amateurs involved tonight. This is a murder enquiry after all.'

I thought the man rude, but Alistair failed to notice. 'We must move,' he said, swinging his attention toward his team of security officers.

I cocked my head to one side, trying not to react but feeling like I had just been dismissed by my own lover. 'Alistair,' I called again to get his attention.

This time he gave me his full attention and reached forward to take my hands in his. 'I'm sorry, Patricia, dear. I really think I should keep this investigation confined to the official team this time.'

He looked sorry about it, which was something, but I had a question. Not for Alistair though, but for Devrani. 'Mr Bharma, can I ask what your initial theory is, please?'

The man shot me a bored look, then indulged me anyway. 'I suspect everyone and no one at this time. Mrs Patel most likely gave her husband a false alibi, the reason for which is not yet clear but I doubt very much they were indulging in marital activities immediately before the show. We know that Irani Patel has been visiting Dayita's cabin and is most likely involved in an affair with her. The captain has advised me that a calling card was used to mark the victim and that the calling cards have been showing up on board the Aurelia for far longer than the pool of likely suspects has been on board. This in itself compounds the mystery though I believe it will be easy enough to solve. The calling card may be that of a professional assassin, brought on board to kill Dayita, which suggests the murder was not only premeditated but also meticulously planned. Alternatively, the calling card may be a ruse to throw us off the scent entirely. I am also aware that a gem from Irani's cufflinks was found near the murder victim. He remains the prime suspect, but I am not one for jumping to conclusions. My investigations will be meticulous and flawless. Whoever the murderer is, whatever the murderer thinks, he will not be able to confound Devrani Bharma. Beyond those initial thoughts, it would be misleading to share anything else with you.' He really did dismiss me at that point, walking away without another word.

Alistair twitched to follow him but stopped to speak with me. 'Patricia, will you be alright? I hate to cut you out…'

I held up a hand to stop him. 'Sweetie, you go have fun with your detective friend. I wish you luck, but he has the whole thing wrong and I am going to prove it.'

Alistair's eyebrows tried to reach the top of his head. 'You have another theory about what is happening?'

'I feel a wager is warranted.' I was throwing down a gauntlet in challenge. How dare Alistair think he can solve a mystery without me? I had his attention though and that of everyone else in earshot as his lieutenants tried to listen without looking like they were. 'I will present you with the name of the murderer before the Aurelia makes port in Mumbai. Your challenge is to correctly identify that person and their motive before I do.'

'And what is the wager?' he asked, a wry smile on his face at being challenged so bare-facedly in front of his crew.

'I'll let you name it if you win, but since you don't stand a chance, I shall name it when I do.' Several of his security team gasped at my audacity and confidence. 'I have just one request,' I added.

'Oh, yes? I'm all ears?' he replied with humour and excitement; the chase was about to be on!

'I may need to access areas I have no right to access or ask questions I have no right to ask in my pursuit of this case. I request you assign me a member of the security team for the next twenty-four hours.' He inclined his head in thought and I thought he might be about to say no when I added, 'I might run into the murderer when I am poking about.'

That made his mind up quickly enough. With a broad sweep of his arm, he indicated all the lieutenants in sight. 'Take your pick, my dear.'

'I volunteer,' said Baker, but he wasn't the only one to step forward. Schneider, Pippin, Bhukari and others all put their hands up or indicated their desire to be on Team Patricia.

I had to laugh. 'Lieutenant Baker it is then. Fastest man wins the job.'

Surprised by his crews' reaction, he asked, 'Why, Baker? Why are you so keen to work with Mrs Fisher?'

Lieutenant Baker's cheeks coloured as he addressed the ship's senior officer. 'Well, sir. No offense intended, of course.'

'Of course,' Alistair echoed.

'Well, Mrs Fisher does seem more likely to solve this...'

'...than me,' the captain finished his lieutenant's sentence, making the man cringe in the process. 'Well, there you have it. Now I will have to prove you all wrong.' He extended his hand. 'Good luck, Mrs Fisher.'

I shook it. 'Good luck, Captain Huntley.'

Then he barked an order and jogged from the ballroom with all the white uniforms hot on his heels. All bar one, that is, as Lieutenant Baker remained with me. Barbie and Jermaine came to join us.

Baker rubbed his hands together, an eager gesture. 'So, Mrs Fisher, who is the killer?'

'I haven't the faintest idea,' I admitted, putting a hand to my forehead as I realised just how far I had allowed my ego to push my luck.

Baker's eyes went from excited and eager to panicked and wide in the space of a heartbeat. 'Um,' he stuttered.

'Don't worry,' said Barbie, clapping him on his arm. 'Patty will figure it all out. Won't you, Patty?'

I joined Baker in saying, 'Um.'

'What about the pregnancy test, madam?' asked Jermaine. 'That is a place to start, is it not?'

I nodded. 'We have some research to do and some questions to ask. Let's get back to my suite.' I started walking, my brain whirling as I tried to work out what I thought. Irani Patel was involved somehow, that I was certain of, but I wasn't sure he was the murderer even though I found an opal from his cufflinks in the murdered girl's cabin and another at the site of her murder. I even had a theory about the calling card; that was something Rick and Akamu were working on – a secret mission that might prove to be a wild goose chase but one which suited their history and skill sets.

'What's in your suite?' asked Baker.

Barbie, Jermaine, and I all paused and turned to look at him, glanced at each other and then, as one, said, 'Gin.'

Gin

I doubted it was a good thing that my perfectly proportioned, size zero, gym instructor friend now drank gin and tonic with me on a semi-regular basis, but it probably wasn't going to do her too much harm either.

Jermaine had set about making drinks as soon as we came though the door. Well, actually, he went about making drinks once we were in the suite but only after we fielded Anna the attack dog as she tried to shred Lieutenant Baker's ankle. She was so mistrustful of anyone she didn't know and would attack on sight without the slightest provocation.

Baker had seen her coming and stopped moving, assuming, incorrectly, that she would just give him a sniff, he then proceeded to yelp and hop about as she bit hold of his trousers. She was so fast and so low to the ground that neither Barbie, Jermaine, nor I had been able to grab her before she got to him. Even after I had forced a finger into her mouth to prise it open and force her to release Baker's leg she continued to stare at him mistrustfully and curl her top lip.

Thankfully, she gave up and went to sleep back on the couch when I told her to stay. Now all four of us were crowded around the computer in my suite, each with a glass filled with ice and the cold refreshing combination of Hendrick's gin and slimline tonic over sliced cucumber.

'That is pretty darned fine,' commented Baker as he tried the drink for the first time ever. Our four glasses clinked together in salute, but it was time to get on with the investigation. 'You were telling me about Dayita being pregnant,' Baker reminded me.

'Might be pregnant,' I corrected him. 'I have a positive pregnancy test and a wrapper from one of the same brand from the bin in her room.'

'How did you get in her room?' Baker asked.

I flapped a dismissive arm at him, not wanting to tell him and about the stolen universal keycard in my handbag. 'Unimportant. The point is, it suggests that Dayita was pregnant but if she is, then we have to discover who the father is. I want to speak with Rajesh first. I think we should bring him here and let Jermaine have a one to one chat with the man. I think it likely that he is indeed gay, in which case I doubt he was actually sleeping with Dayita and therefore isn't the father.'

'Why would he go to such trouble to hide his sexuality?' Barbie asked.

I shrugged. 'Some countries are less enlightened about such things. As I understand it, India only changed the law to make homosexuality legal a few years ago.'

Beside me Jermaine tapped a few keys on the computer. 'It was last September,' he read from the screen. He sounded as surprised as I felt.

'That recent?' I questioned, leaning over his shoulder to read it myself. 'No wonder he is reluctant to make it public.'

Jermaine nodded. 'It must be tough to come out publicly in a country that was still persecuting people for their lifestyles so recently.'

'Okay,' said Barbie. 'So, if we assume Rajesh isn't the father, perhaps he will know who is.' She patted Jermaine's shoulder. 'I know I share things with my gay BFF that I don't necessarily share even with other girls.'

'That's true,' acknowledged Jermaine.

Baker got what they were saying. 'So, if Dayita was having an affair with someone… say a married man or the host of the show, then the one person she might have told about it, is Rajesh.'

Barbie nodded. 'That would be a good place to start.'

Baker knocked back the last of his gin and tonic and placed the glass on the kitchen counter with a meaningful thump. 'Let's get to that after party then. We ought to be able to find him there.'

'Anna!' My little dog was still asleep on the couch, but her head came up when I called her name. 'Let's go, girl.' At my beckoning, she leapt nimbly from the couch, performed a stretch, which on a creature which already looks to have been stretched by nature, is quite a sight, then trotted across the room to the door where everyone else was gathering.

Then she coughed; a delightful hacking sound that make me wonder if she was about to retch.

'Is she okay?' asked Barbie.

I stared down at the dog. She stared back up at me, but she didn't cough again so I figured it was just a dog thing.

Jermaine clipped her lead onto her collar and handed it to me. Then the five of us went out to solve a mystery.

Where's Rajesh?

I wasn't sure what to expect at the after party. The cast and crew ought to be in a party mood because they were on a luxurious cruise ship and had just been part of the biggest television show in the history of their country. It would make the stars of the show even bigger stars and make stars out of those that weren't already. The crew might be in for bonuses; I genuinely didn't know if that was how these things worked, but were it not for Dayita's murder, one could expect everyone involved in the show to now be letting their hair down.

The party had an additional guest list which was again made up using a lottery draw to determine who got a ticket. The numbers to attend were about one third of those who were able to attend the live show in the ballroom and there were some crew included in the draw again. There were television cameras at the after party, recording the cast of the show as they discussed how tonight had gone and talked about what would happen next week. I learned that this was a regular feature of the show in whichever country it was shown and that tickets to get to the after party each week were seriously hot stuff.

Dayita had been murdered though and that must be having an effect on everyone involved in the TV show even if they were not close to her. It was a grisly death too, not that I thought the details had been leaked, but a lake of blood from under the door of a toilet stall would spark rumours fast enough.

So, coming into the party, I wasn't sure what to expect, but it wasn't what I found: no one seemed bothered about the murder of one of their colleagues.

That is probably misleading, but what I mean is that there was no visible sign that anyone was mourning. Two members of the security team were wearing their finest white uniform to greet guests and check tickets. There ensued a brief discussion as Jermaine and Barbie did not have tickets and I hadn't bothered to bring mine, but Baker didn't need much time to convince them that we were going inside whether they let us or not.

Once inside, the smiles and laughter I could see and hear from outside was proven to be the theme throughout. The dancers and stars were mostly in their pairs, their matching outfits making them easy to spot. I also spotted members of the television crew mingling in the crowd. Everyone was in ball gowns and dinner jackets with the exception of Alistair, who stood out because of his white uniform and one or two other members of crew who were also in the cruise line's livery.

Alistair spotted me and detached himself from Devrani Bharma to come my way. I fixed a smile to my face and through it said, 'Spilt up and find Rajesh,' to my three companions. Wordlessly, they each changed direction at the same time, splitting off to search the room full of people.

There were camera crews going about and two new hosts with handheld microphones who were tracking down people to speak with.

Alistair arrived and leaned in to kiss my cheek, narrowly avoiding a lick from Anna as he came close to her. One of the hosts spotted us and swung their attention our way bringing a camera with them. 'Figured it out yet?' asked Alistair, teasing me deliberately.

'I'll let you know when I do,' I replied, then smiled as the host, a tall, lean and very attractive woman in her thirties pushed a microphone towards us.

'Who do we have here then? The captain of the ship if I am not mistaken, Captain Alistair Huntley.' She had clearly done her homework.

'Tell me, Captain, how wonderful was it having such a successful show on board your ship?'

It was a leading question, the interviewer clearly expecting a positive response. Alistair, of course, provided exactly what was required. 'It was incredible,' he gushed. 'The pageantry, the flamboyance, it was incredible.' I knew he was doing what his employers expected of him, but it still felt a little false. I smiled at the camera nevertheless and showed them my teeth as he continued. 'My crew are proud and privileged to have the stars of Indian television on board. Purple Star Cruise Lines are the premier carrier for all passengers looking for luxurious sea travel and the quality of this show epitomises the standard that we set in everything that we do.'

The woman smiled deeply as she got the response that she wanted and thrust the microphone under his nose again. 'And who is your lovely companion?'

I spoke for myself rather than being spoken for. 'I am Patricia Fisher, a guest on board the Aurelia and a friend of the captain.'

'Looks like you might be more than a friend?' the woman teased. I had no idea how to respond to her taunt, so I smiled; I couldn't think of anything else to do. I wanted to turn away or tell her to move on but with the camera pointed at me, neither option seemed viable.

Alistair rescued me. 'Patricia is the lady staying in the most prestigious suite on the world's most luxurious cruise ship. As such she deserves particularly special treatment and is to be considered a jewel to be treasured aboard the ship.' He delivered the line without the slightest sense of irony and gave my waist a squeeze to impart that he meant every word. Not for the first time in his presence, he made my heart swell.

'Goodness,' the host remarked. She actually looked taken aback by his statement. Then she turned her own face to the camera and addressed the audience wherever they were, 'The fantasy of love is alive and well here, ladies and gentlemen. Is it the majesty of the show? You be the judge, but whatever you do, make sure you vote for your favourite couple.' The man holding the camera showed clear and lowered it, rolling his shoulder to push some life back into it as a demonstration that his job was tougher than it looked.

The pretty Indian woman's smile fell the second the camera was off her face, almost as if the muscles in her face had been cut. Then she rubbed her cheeks, massaging some life back into them. 'God, I can't feel my face anymore. You would not believe how hard it is; smiling all the time, I swear, I want to pull my teeth out some days.' Then, almost before she had finished talking to us, she spotted someone else she wanted to interview, and her smile was fixed back in place as she rushed off with one hand snatching at the collar of her cameraman's shirt.

'She was fun,' I commented as she dashed away from us.

Alistair hung his head. 'Sometimes I wonder if the price I pay for my captaincy is too high.' I understood what he was saying; the political game would tire me very quickly. He shook it off and turned me to face him. 'I thought you were hot on the trail of the killer. What are you doing here?'

'Looking for someone. What is your master detective doing?'

'Observing.' Alistair looked about for Devrani, finding him across the room by himself. 'He says that the killer will reveal himself.'

'Himself? He has decided the killer is a man?'

'Apparently. He is very methodical.'

Barbie swung back into view, heading my way with a disappointed look on her face. 'I can't find him,' she said as she got to me.

'Who are you looking for?' asked Alistair.

I frowned at him. 'Never you mind, Mr Nosey.'

Jermaine appeared as well, quickly followed by Lieutenant Baker. Both had struck out as well. 'No one has seen him,' said Baker. 'I checked with the chaps on the door and they don't think he came in yet.'

I spotted Taginda and set off for her. She looked utterly unbothered by the tragic events of the evening, talking animatedly with a small group and commanding their attention. 'Have you seen Rajesh anywhere?' I asked, butting in rudely.

She shot me a look with daggers in. 'No. Why?'

'He's not here.'

'So?'

I sagged with exasperation. 'Taginda, do you not care about him at all? You made him feel vulnerable and exposed and now no one knows where he is.'

She put her hands on her hips as she rounded on me, taking a pace forward to get into my personal space. 'I'm not responsible for him. He's no longer my dance partner so I don't care where he is.'

It was clear to me that I would gain nothing by wasting further time speaking with the awful woman. I left her where she was, rejoining my friends and herding them toward the door. 'If he's not here, there's no point hanging around. We need to find him.'

'There's a lot of ship to search,' Baker pointed out.

Barbie held up her phone. 'Someone must have a number for him.'

I scanned around and spotted the producer, still carrying the clipboard and still working while everyone else appeared to now be relaxing. 'Let's ask her.' I had to weave through crowds of guests to get to her and Baker got there first. By the time I joined him he had already broached the subject.

'No, I haven't seen him,' the woman was saying. 'I do have a number for him though.' She took out her own phone and used it to call him. The phone was pressed to her ear but when she didn't speak and moved the phone to look at the screen again, I was unsurprised when she said, 'No answer.'

I thanked her, got Barbie to take down his number so we could try again later and considered my next move. 'We'll find Rajesh soon enough, I'm sure. I want to visit Dr Kim. Dayita's body will have been moved to the morgue by now. He may be able to tell us more.'

The Morgue

I tried not to dwell on the fact that I knew my way to the ship's morgue without having to look for directions; I had been there several times since I came on board. We were mostly silent on the way there, most of the journey spent in an elevator to get down into the bowels of the ship. The one thing we did discuss was the calling card and the indentations, trying once more to work out what could be going on. We got no further with it though.

At the door to the morgue, Lieutenant Baker knocked. We could hear voices coming from the other side of the door, which opened a few seconds later to reveal Dr Kim's face.

'Lieutenant Baker, good evening.' Dr Kim stepped back to let us file in. He was with a colleague, one of the other doctors, but I didn't know his name.

I stepped forward to meet him. 'Hello. I'm Patricia Fisher,' I introduced myself and offered my hand to shake.

He pulled his hand back, offering an apology instead. 'Sorry. I need to clean this before I touch anyone. I have just been examining our poor murder victim. I'm Dr David Davis, by the way.'

'What are you able to tell us?' Baker asked.

Dr Kim came around from closing the door to join the rest of us. Across the room, a sheet was draped over a still form; that of Dayita I assumed. Dr Davis turned on taps and began scrubbing his hands. Over his shoulder, he said, 'The victim was stabbed only once. The knife penetrating her left ventricle to kill her instantly. It wasn't a frenzied attack and the victim has no other wounds, not even defensive marks to her hands which one might expect. I think we can assume she knew the killer and wasn't expecting the attack.'

Dr Kim spoke up, 'That's conjecture, Dr Davis.'

Dr Davis nodded. 'It is. Lieutenant Baker is conducting a murder enquiry though, isn't he? Therefore, I plan to tell him what assumptions I can draw from my autopsy.' He finished scrubbing his hands and began to dry them. 'I always fancied solving a crime by finding clues in the victim's wounds. I loved that old TV show, Quincey.'

'Yes, well. I think we should stick to the facts,' Dr Kim chided.

His hands now dry, Dr Davis turned to face us, then pointed to the body. 'Would you like to see?'

'Eww, no thanks,' answered Barbie, instantly backing away.

I wrinkled my nose in equal displeasure but nodded anyway. 'If it will help me to understand what happened to her, then yes.'

Soberly, Dr Davis crossed the room, Dr Kim, me, and Lieutenant Baker following. At the examining table, he peeled back the sheet to reveal Dayita's naked body. There were stitches holding her together where Dr Davis had cut her apart to examine her. It was horrible to look at and I cursed myself for thinking I ought to be brave. This would stay with me now and it was far worse because I had seen her alive and vibrant just a few hours ago.

'The knife entered her chest here.' Dr Davis indicated using a small silver utensil. 'The thrust was going down, indicating that the victim was most likely in a seated position with the killer standing over her.' He mimed an overhand downward thrust - the famous slashing knife from *Psycho* flashed across my memory.

'What's that mark there?' Baker asked pointing to her chest.

'Ah, yes. That's a condition called polymastia.' When Baker and I stared at him with blank expressions he added, 'A third nipple. It's quite rare.'

'It doesn't look like a nipple,' Baker argued.

It was high on her right breast and about an inch from where the knife's blade had entered. Dr Davis leaned over her for a closer look and pointed to it with the utensil again. 'If you look closely you can see the lactiferous duct. It is a supernumerary nipple so wouldn't actually work – there is no milk supply to it, but I can assure you that is what it is. It's only the second one I have ever seen myself. How about you Dr Kim?'

Dr Kim shifted to look at the nipple as well. 'It occurs most often in family lines. I have seen several but that's because I grew up with a boy that had one. Everyone in his family did and it went back many generations. I never found out if he passed it on to his children though.'

The nipple was interesting but insignificant to the case. 'Where is the card?' I asked.

'Ah yes.' Dr Davis crossed to a locker where evidence bags were stored. In them would be her clothes and any other personal items he found on her. In a small plastic bag, he held aloft the white calling card. It wasn't very white anymore; the knife had gone right through the middle of it. I remembered seeing it pinned to her with the signature and brush stroke uppermost.

Baker asked, 'What else can you tell us?'

'As it pertains to her murder? Not much.'

'Was she pregnant?' I asked the question I thought important.

Dr Davis nodded again. 'Yes, about eight weeks. Approximately.'

I had another question now, 'Is it possible to use DNA to determine who the father is?'

Dr Davis looked surprised by the question but answered anyway. 'Yes. But not here. We don't have the equipment to do that. It is probably something that can be determined by the police in Mumbai though. You would need a list of suspects first though unless you plan to test every man on the planet.'

I thought about that. The natural assumption here was that Dayita was sleeping with Irani Patel and therefore he was the father. Something about that felt wrong though and I still couldn't work out what the calling card had to do with it all.

Behind me, Anna hacked again, the awful sound like she was going to vomit coming for the third or fourth time now. Jermaine, who was holding her lead, bent down to pick her up.

'Is she okay?' I asked.

He was peering into her mouth as she hacked again. 'I think she has something caught in her teeth.'

Barbie was peering into her mouth as well now, the little dog fighting them both as Barbie tried to hold her jaws open. I joined them, adding my voice to calm the struggling Dachshund, 'Anna, just let mummy see.'

She was disinclined to play along though, almost slipping from Jermaine's grasp in her determination to get away. She weighed less than ten pounds and her legs were shorter than my fingers, but she could wriggle and fight like you wouldn't believe.

The three of us manoeuvred her to an empty examining table and managed to pin her down. Finally, with Jermaine holding her back end, Barbie holding her head and with my fingers inside her mouth, I hooked the thing that was making her gag and yanked it free.

A soggy, disgusting piece of red cotton had caught on her teeth and had been trailing down her throat to make her gag and cough. I looked about for a bin to throw it in but then stopped myself.

Where had it come from?

'Jermaine, has she been chewing anything red?' I couldn't think of anything I owned in this shade.

'No, madam. I do not believe so.'

Anna was still wriggling to be set free. I met her eyes. 'Where did you get this, Anna?' I got no answer of course, she licked her lips instead as Jermaine let her up and popped her on the floor. 'Do you have an evidence bag?' I asked. The question was aimed at the doctors, but Lieutenant Baker produced one from a pocket before either man could move.

I dropped the offensive piece of red cotton into the bag, having to flick my fingers to convince it to come off it was so stuck on with doggy dribble. Then I gave my hands a good scrub. Itching away at the back of my head was a feeling that I was missing something. Something to do with the mysterious calling cards and what they were all about. I needed to spend more time looking at the suites in which the cards had been found, compile a list of dates and who the passengers were and where they had been when the mysterious calling card bandit got into their cabins.

'Baker, can you get us a plan of the ship? Specifically the top deck?'

'Err, yeah, probably,' he shrugged.

I dried my hands on a towel and started back toward the door. I was done with the morgue and poor Dayita. 'We need to get back to my suite. There's work to do.'

Jermaine gave Anna's lead a little tug and fell in step behind me, but none of us got to the door. A call came through the radio to Dr Kim and we all heard it. 'Dr Kim, this is Lieutenant Boyns. Can you come to the gentleman's toilets outside the upper deck restaurant? There's another body.'

Mystery Solved

We raced to the elevator, all six of us wasting no time as we hurried to find out who the latest victim was. Drs Kim and Davis grabbed medical bags as they ran out the door but caught up to the rest of us at the elevator doors. Little Anna, propelled by the sudden excitement, was scrabbling on the deck with her claws as she tried to run faster than Jermaine's tight grip on her lead would allow.

Once on the upper deck, we slowed our pace as there were passengers about, but still walked as fast as we could. Right back at the restaurant, still looking like a ballroom and ready for the results show the following night, white uniforms were waiting for the doctors to arrive. The ladies' toilet, where Dayita had been found just a few hours ago, was still cordoned off with a solitary guard standing outside it. No doubt there was still evidence to be gathered inside. Now though, the focus of activity was on the gentlemens' toilet twenty feet further down the passageway.

Dr Kim went straight inside, followed by Dr Davis. I doubted both were needed but the call had come to them and they had both reacted as one. Lieutenant Baker also went inside but I hesitated by the door.

'Is it Rajesh?' I asked, calling loudly enough for those inside to hear me and answer.

Baker's voice came back with the answer and the mystery of the missing man's whereabouts had been solved. Barbie, Jermaine and I exchanged a grim look and I steeled myself to head inside. I didn't particularly want to see the man's body, but it was probably necessary if I planned to catch his killer.

The gents' toilet was more or less a complete copy of the ladies' toilet next door. There were fewer cubicles though and a wall of urinals instead.

Right at the end of the row of stalls, Dr Kim was staring in through the open door. It was the same stall that Dayita had been found in, just in a different toilet.

Forcing my feet to move though they felt wobbly and light, I approached the stall and looked in. Rajesh was propped against the toilet but sitting on the floor. His head was at an unnatural angle and his mouth was open to reveal that something had been shoved in it.

'It's another calling card,' Baker told me before I could ask. I could see it now, the rectangular shape of the white card protruding from between his lips. His trousers and underwear were pulled down and his shirt was hanging open though it looked like it had been ripped rather than carefully undone. Around his throat I could see bruising – he had been strangled. That, at least, was my guess though I was sure the doctors would confirm it one way or another soon enough.

Echoing through the door, I heard the familiar voice of the captain approaching. I moved away to the side as he came in; I had seen enough.

'Patricia.' He gave me a grim smile as he came into the room. Grim smiles were a favourite this evening it seemed.

I nodded at him. 'Alistair.'

Devrani Bharma swept into the toilet as well with Schneider and Bhukari hot on his heels. He paid me no attention but the room was getting too full now so I left. There was nothing more for me to do in there anyway. Another person had been killed and another calling card used to mark the body. What on earth was going on? Was he killed to prevent him revealing something about Dayita? I wanted to question him about his relationship with her, but I couldn't do that now. Whatever he knew had gone with him. I suspected, but couldn't be certain, that he was the one that had tipped me off about her pregnancy. I couldn't prove it either way now.

I joined Barbie and Jermaine, the three of us waiting quietly until Baker also joined us. 'Can you get that plan of the upper deck?' I asked him. 'We'll meet you in my suite.'

We set off in different directions with a plan to meet up again as soon as possible. As we wandered back to my suite, Barbie said, 'Someone sure has it in for this show.'

It was her comment that sparked the idea in my head. Something linked the different parts of this mystery. I didn't know what it was yet, but I didn't think it was the show, or sex. There was something else.

A Pattern

Once back in my own space, I kicked my shoes off and wriggled my toes around. I liked the extra height they gave me, but the fabulous shoes from the Philippines became uncomfortable quite quickly. Jermaine went to the kitchen to prepare some food and Barbie sat herself down on the couch. Anna immediately joined her, seeing someone with a lap that could make a fuss of her and not thinking twice about it.

'Have you had your allergy meds?' I asked her.

She nodded as she stroked Anna's coat, the dog instantly rolling over to have her tummy rubbed. 'Yeah, the stuff Dr Kim gave me really works.'

I crossed to the desk where I grabbed a pad and started trying to order my thoughts. There had been two murders in a single evening. Two dancers from the same television show that were supposedly a couple. As I wrote down their names and drew a line between them, Barbie gently rolled Anna onto a cushion and came to join me.

'May I offer you a beverage, madam?' called Jermaine from the kitchen. I popped my head up, argued with the gin demon and asked for a pot of tea instead. I was going to need a clear head to stay on top of what was going on. Gin could come later.

'What else do we know?' Barbie asked, leaning on the desk to see what I had written.

'Dayita was stabbed but I think Dr Kim will show that Rajesh was strangled.' I wrote down, *changing methods* and underlined it.

'Both of them had calling cards on them,' said Jermaine joining us with a tray of crockery.

Barbie looked at me. 'What do you make of that?'

I shook my head and pursed my lips. 'I'm not sure.'

She leaned across to tap the mouse and slid into the chair in front of the keyboard. 'If the calling cards have been appearing for two weeks longer than the dancers have been on board, then the murderer leaving the calling cards cannot be anyone from the show.' She made a valid point.

'Could it be someone with a grudge against the show?' asked Jermaine, back in the kitchen and pouring hot water into my teapot.

'I want to ignore the calling cards,' I said, scribbling out the words on my pad.

'How come?' asked Barbie.

'Because they don't fit.'

Barbie gave me a confused look, letting me know she thought I was getting it wrong. 'But the killer left them behind,' she pointed out. 'They killed two people in the space of a few hours and left a token on each victim so everyone would know who the killer was.'

'But we don't know who the killer is,' I argued. 'We are just as baffled as we would be if no calling card had been left. Possibly less so, actually.'

Jermaine arrived with the tea and began filling cups. 'I'm with Barbie on this one, madam. I am struggling to follow your logic. Do you believe that the discovery of the calling cards is coincidental or misleading?'

Both my companions were looking at me, waiting for my answer. I didn't have one though. It made sense that whoever was leaving the cards was also the killer. The person had been breaking into suites for the last couple of weeks at least but I didn't know what that person was doing in the suites. If they were connected to the dancing show, then how?

A knock at the door rescued me from trying to explain my thoughts any further and had I wanted to, I would have needed to shout to be heard over Anna's latest cacophony of barking. Adept now at dealing with my ferocious attack hound, Jermaine simply scooped her under one arm as he answered the door.

Lieutenant Baker strode purposefully in carrying a long cardboard tube. 'I managed to find this,' he announced, holding it aloft as Jermaine put Anna back on the floor. Despite looking calm, she launched once more into attack mode and went for Baker's ankles again.

He uttered a rude word and blushed as he attempted to fend her off with the cardboard tube and succeeded only in getting it chewed. 'Sorry,' he blushed again as I took my turn in dealing with the mental Dachshund.

'That's perfectly alright,' I assured him. It wasn't as if I hadn't heard the word before. 'What have you got for us?'

'A plan of the upper deck.' He checked his left, right and behind for any further sign of attack, then pulled a plastic stopper from the end of the long tube and shook the contents out onto my dining table.

Jermaine fetched ornaments and a plant pot to pin down the plan as Baker rolled it out. It was longer than the six foot long table and hung off both ends but showed a slice of the ship with all of the cabins, storerooms, restaurants, Barbie's gym and everything else marked clearly and to scale.

Once it was flat, Baker pulled a tablet from a trouser side pocket. 'I also have a list of which suites have reported the discovery of a calling card and when.' The next few minutes was spent marking carefully on the plan which suites had been targeted. We did that using little sticky notes rather than ruin the beautiful and exact plan with a marker pen. When finished though, we stood back and looked at our handiwork.

Barbie said what we were all thinking. 'It's a pattern.'

The suites were arranged around the outside of the ship. Entrance doors ran down a pair of corridors, one on the portside and one to starboard so that each suite was accessed from the inside of the ship and had a balcony or sea view or, in my case, an entire sun terrace. The person leaving the calling cards had started in the middle, targeting the four suites sitting directly amidships. Then they had jumped out two suites and gone aft of the port side. The next to be targeted was the suite two suites up on the starboard side toward the prow. It continued like that. There were some holes which we put down to the crime never being reported – this seemed likely since nothing was ever taken. However, having identified a pattern, we could predict, to some degree of accuracy, which suite would be next in line.

I felt a grin stretching the corners of my mouth. The calling card criminal had been operating earlier today, targeting both my suite and Irani Patel's so the next suite, if the pattern persisted, was on the other side of the ship and almost all the way to the stern.

'Who is in that suite?' I asked, jabbing the plan with a finger. Jermaine slid into the seat by the computer and clicked the mouse to bring it to life.

Lieutenant Baker glanced up, did a double take and sucked in a breath. 'Are you accessing the ship's central registry?' he asked.

I gave him a sideways look. 'Of course.'

'But that's for crew only. Passengers are not supposed to ever have access to it.' He was shaking his head, the dutiful security officer suddenly finding himself on the wrong side of an invisible line.

'How do you think we solved half the crimes over the last few weeks?' I scoffed.

Barbie moved in next to Jermaine to see what came up on the screen but looked back at Baker over her shoulder. 'Don't worry, we never let Patty see the screen.'

'Really?' he asked, surprised but also sounding relieved.

Barbie laughed. 'No. Of course not really. How would we manage that? She's the sleuth here. Jermaine's the muscle, I get to be the pretty girl and Patty is the brain.'

'What does that make me?' he asked.

'That depends on you?' she teased. 'You might be the plucky hero in the dashing uniform, swooping in at the last moment to perform the official bit and make an arrest.' He liked the sound of that, a satisfied smile curling across his face. 'Or you might be the boring, stick in the mud official with a badge that spoils all the fun and tells tales about using the ship's central registry system to stop a killer.' His smile fell and he grumpily tucked his bottom lip in as he too went over to see what information the computer had for us.

Barbie gave him a nudge so he would know she was teasing but he read from the screen. 'Vihann Veghale. Is he one of the television stars?'

'He sure is.' I had met him earlier. A tall and handsome man and another star of Bollywood movies known for his good looks. He was one of the bigger stars on the show if his position on the posters displayed around the ship were anything to go on.

'Was he at the party earlier?' I creased my brow in thought, trying to picture whether I had seen him or not. 'I don't remember,' I concluded. I hadn't been looking for him and had mostly been distracted by Alistair and the host woman.

Baker slid his tablet back into a pocket and checked his sidearm was secure; he looked ready to go somewhere. 'I think we should check to see if his suite is safe, don't you?' he asked, taking a pace toward the door.

I nodded. It made sense to just keep rolling forward. 'What if he is at the party?' Barbie asked. 'He might have been there when we were. I didn't know to look for him.'

'Or he might have arrived late,' added Jermaine.

I looked at Baker. 'It's just around the corner and a deck down. We might as well check there first.' I couldn't present a reason why we shouldn't so the four of us all set off again. I really wanted to put some comfortable shoes on, or maybe a pair of flip flops. I was going back to a room filled with people in ball gowns and dinner jackets though, so grumpily, I stuffed my feet back into my high-heeled dancing shoes again.

Anna, sitting on the couch, made not the slightest move to follow us as we went out the door, undoubtedly grateful to be getting left behind for once. It would make my life easier too.

Or would it?

Vihaan Veghale

Back at the after party, the crowd appeared to be enjoying themselves. There was no sense that two people had been murdered. How was it that nobody seemed to be upset?

I spotted one of the dancers, the one that had challenged Taginda and forced her to reveal what she said when she learned of Dayita's death earlier. She was talking with another pair of dancers and her own dance partner, who I then recognised as Vihann Veghale. I went straight over to them.

'Hi, everyone.' I waved my hello as I joined their group. It was a mix of celebrities and dancers and some of the passengers who were talking with them. The television personalities were being great hosts, mingling with the passengers and really selling the show. The conversation paused as they turned my way. Helpfully, Lieutenant Baker arrived at my side just as everyone was waiting for me to speak. 'I was hoping I might borrow Vihaan and his dance partner?' I said it as a question, offering them an engaging smile in the hope that they would voluntarily split from the group to speak with me.

Vihaan's eyebrows flickered in question, wondering who I was and what I might want, but he took a step toward me as the group closed their circle and began speaking again. 'How can I help you, Miss...?'

'Patricia. I'm Patricia Fisher.' I swept my arm to include the man in uniform to my right. 'This is Lieutenant Baker of the ship's security team.'

Away from the attention of other people his diminutive dance partner, Arabella, allowed her face to show the emotions she was trying to bury. Grief surfaced fleetingly but was gone almost as quickly.

'Are you Dayita's roommate?' I asked the small woman.

Her face crumpled slightly as she fought for control but buried her head into Vihaan's side as a tear escaped. He comforted her as she snivelled her reply, 'I was.'

I pursed my lips. This was difficult. Vihaan ignored me to address his colleague. 'Are you alright, Arabella? Would you like to leave?' She shook her head and he turned his attention back to me. 'This is a difficult time for all of us, Mrs Fisher. Is there a good reason for your intrusion?'

He was protecting Arabella, I respected him for that, but now I had to quiz him about his suite. 'You're staying in the Kensington Suite, are you not?' He shot me an inquiring look, more curious now that I knew personal details about him. 'I ask because there has been a series of break ins to the suites on the upper deck and I can reliably predict that yours will be next.' His eyes flared in surprise at my announcement. 'It may even have already occurred.'

Arabella pushed herself upright to face us for the first time. 'Someone is going to break into his rooms? Why?'

Lieutenant Baker answered her, 'We don't know yet. The motivation does not appear to be theft but whoever is doing it may also be mixed up in the murders this evening.'

'Murders?' Arabella echoed, her voice coming out as a startled shout.

Lieutenant Baker closed his eyes in horror; he had just blurted the news of the second murder and every conversation within a ten-yard radius had stopped instantly at Arabella's cry.

It was too late now, so I stepped in close to Arabella and Vihaan. 'I think it is important that we check your suite, Vihaan. Can you come with us?'

'No.' He swiped my encouraging arm away as I reached toward him. 'Who else has been murdered?' I kept my mouth shut as I tried to work out what my best move was at this point. We were attracting attention, more people gravitating towards as us Vihaan caused a scene. 'Who else?' he demanded.

Lieutenant Baker saved me. 'Sir, I'm afraid I cannot give you that information. An official announcement will be made.'

'It's Rajesh!' The shout came from Taginda. 'It's Rajesh, isn't it?' Suddenly everyone was looking around in a desperate bid to find him.

Arabella looked horrified. 'Oh, my goodness. What happened to Rajesh.'

I didn't have a chance to answer though, Taginda was creating too much noise. 'I knew it!' she screamed. 'I knew one of you would make sure I didn't win! That's why he never showed up at the after party. That's why I have been by myself since I got here. One of you killed him!'

Arabella's mouth dropped open and she pushed away from Vihaan as he scrambled to contain her. She had daggers for eyes and was heading straight for Taginda. 'You think this is about you?'

'Isn't it?' Taginda snapped back at her.

'You think someone went to the trouble of killing your dance partner just to stop you winning this stupid competition? Why would they do that when it would be doing the world a service if they just killed you?' There were gasps at Arabella's outburst, but I could see there were plenty of people that didn't necessarily disagree.

Taginda though, was horrified. 'Was it you? Did you kill Rajesh? You hate me, everyone knows it.' She was pointing a finger at Arabella and waving it, getting everyone's attention. 'Someone arrest her.'

Baker lifted his arms in a bid to stifle the riot before it happened. 'Listen. Listen, please. No one said that Rajesh is the second murder victim.'

'But there is a second murder victim, isn't there?' Vihaan pointed out. Again, poor Baker closed his eyes in horror; he wasn't doing very well.

As far as I was concerned the cat was out of the bag. I still needed to speak with Vihaan though and I wanted to get his room open and see if we could set a trap for the calling card criminal. Catching that person would go a long way to solving this crime spree and would answer a whole lot of questions.

I stepped right into his personal space so I could speak with him quietly. 'We need to see if your room has been broken into, Vihaan. It's important. We don't know if the person breaking into the suites is involved in the murders or not, but if we can catch them...' I could see in his eyes that he wanted to argue. 'Tell me, have you found a small white business card on your nightstand?'

His questioning look gave me my answer. 'A business card?'

'Yes.' Baker had heard his question and guessed what I had been telling him. 'It would look like this?' He produced a card from his pocket to show the man.

'And that would have been on my nightstand?' Vihaan asked.

'Only if the criminal has already broken into your suite. I take it you are telling us that you haven't found one. This is good news,' I added before he could comment.

'Can you take us to your suite, sir?' asked Baker.

Around us, the crowd were looking surly. The security guys from the entrance had moved in to calm people down but everyone was demanding information and Taginda was still pointing her finger at anyone that challenged her.

I'm not sure Vihaan wanted to take us to his suite, but he certainly didn't want to stay where he was. The lucky passengers that had won tickets to the after party were onboard the Aurelia for a holiday, and in many cases, for the holiday of a lifetime. Now they were escaping out of the door, their choice to abandon the party and the chance to mingle with stars of film and television probably a wise one; the party was already over.

With a nod of his head, Baker helped Vihaan and Arabella to slip through the crowd and out of the door. Barbie and Jermaine slipped out right on my heels. We were all heading to the Kensington Suite at the far end of the ship, where we would set a trap to see if we could catch the calling card criminal.

Lies

Arabella tried to quiz Lieutenant Baker on the walk to Vihaan's suite. She wanted to know what had happened to Rajesh and she was crying for her friends. Dayita and Rajesh were both on the professional dancer side of the show and she had known them for some time it seemed. I knew very little about the show, but I knew it had been running for several years with Irani Patel at the helm from the start. He had already been a huge name in India but was even bigger now that he was being seen by millions of viewers every week. Dayita, Arabella, Rajesh and others had all become household names through the show but what would become of them now? Would the show survive this tragedy?

For his part, Lieutenant Baker refused to divulge anything further regarding Rajesh's murder and the circumstances in which he was found. It was the right thing to do, but it frustrated Arabella and Vihaan alike, both of whom wanted to know more about what had happened and why we wouldn't tell them anything.

By the time we reached Vihaan's suite, he was becoming angry. 'You ask for my help and tell me you wish to use my suite to catch a person who, for all I know, is responsible for murdering two people this evening. I demand to know what happened to Rajesh.'

Arabella found her voice too. 'How is it that you are involved in this anyway?' She pointed at Baker. 'He looks like he belongs here. He even has a gun. But that guy looks like a butler.' She nodded at Jermaine. 'I don't understand. Why isn't it a team from the ship's security that are trying to catch the killer?'

We had arrived at the entrance to his suite, but he was making no attempt to open the door for us. I think the question Arabella raised hadn't occurred to him until now but suddenly he was folding his arms across his chest and staring at us like we had no right to be there.

Once again, Baker stepped up to the plate. 'Sir, I am here in my official capacity as an officer of this ship. Mrs Fisher is a special consultant employed by the cruise line.' Not even slightly true. 'And Special Ratings Clarke and Berkeley are her assistants. We have an investigation to conduct which we hope to conclude quickly so that no further harm comes to anyone on board. You can assist with this by giving us free entry to your suite, or I can choose to access it myself in my official capacity.' He paused to let the information sink in. Then added, 'I would rather the former than the latter, sir.'

Baker had been polite and his argument was reasonable even if underpinned with a threat that he would do it anyway. I could see Vihaan trying to work himself up to argue again, but his spirit wasn't in it. There was a criminal to catch; failing to help us in our investigation was just helping the murderer get away.

Wordlessly, he pulled his keycard from a pocket and beeped his door open. We filed in directly after him, sweeping Arabella along with us in our desire to see if the calling card criminal had indeed struck. His suite was much smaller than mine and didn't come with a live-in butler, but it still had a grand living area with couches and a piano and an open plan kitchen. It was decorated with posters from the man's career; gaudy Bollywood posters in large frames, each with Vihaan's face taking centre stage as the star of whichever particular production. He must have brought them on with him or insisted the television crew do so. It suggested an ego that required constant pandering.

I took only a second to take them all in and spot what I had been looking for; the large oil painting I was sure would hide the safe. My feet took me toward it even as Baker peeled off to head into Vihaan's bedroom, leading the suite's principle with Barbie and Arabella following them.

The thing that I hoped I wouldn't find was visible the moment I got past the couch. On the floor, in the carpet, were four small indentations and beyond them was a line of dust. In the bedroom would be a small white calling card on Vihaan's right-side nightstand. We had missed our quarry, but only this time. There would be another opportunity; we just needed to work out which was the next cabin in the pattern. This time it had been easy, but it ended a circuit of cabins so had been obvious. The next target could be any one of about a dozen different cabins, but I was certain the ship had the resources to accommodate setting that many traps. If that was what it took.

There was conversation coming from the bedroom, though I couldn't make out what was being said. No doubt they were staring at the calling card and trying to calm down Vihaan. I remembered how I had reacted to knowledge that someone had been in my bedroom: it was an uncomfortable feeling.

I turned to join them and bumped directly into Jermaine's chest; my silent sentinel; my protection when I needed it, had snuck up behind me. Up until that point, I hadn't realised how on edge I was, but the sudden and unexpected presence of a large man so close to me caused my heart to skip. As I put a hand to my heart, I collapsed into him, laying my head on his chest for comfort and then he did something unexpected and put his arms around me.

My standoffish, staid butler, with his fake English accent and Downton Abbey mannerisms was hugging me. I felt instantly comforted and safe. It was a strange experience in some respects, but in many ways, I also felt like I knew Jermaine as well as I had ever known any man. We only stayed like that for a second or so, but it was a moment that would stay with me forever.

'There's no card.' The sound of Barbie's voice broke our moment, Jermaine taking a respectful pace back as he dropped his arms away from me, but the words shocked me. I peered around Jermaine's side as he stepped away; Barbie was back in the room and Baker was coming through the door behind her.

'Really?' Until I saw their faces, I thought it was a joke or something. They meant it though; there was no calling card in the bedroom. How could that be? I opened my mouth to start arguing; behind me there were indentations in the carpet and a line of dust. I was prepared to state that I knew the calling card criminal had been in this suite, but Jermaine's eyes stopped me. He caught me with his gaze, a meaningful look that silently demanded I stop, and then, when I paused to lock eyes with him, he shook his head. It was an almost imperceptible gesture but one that carried real weight. He had something to tell me, but now wasn't the time.

He broke eye contact before anyone noticed.

'Really,' said Baker. He looked as disappointed as I felt. 'There's nothing there. What have you got?'

My eyes went to Vihaan as he too came out of the bedroom. I had to get a grip on myself and I walked over the top of the indentations so that Barbie and Baker wouldn't see them. 'So, you don't think anyone has been in here?'

Vihaan shook his head. 'It would seem not. Does that mean you can set the trap to catch them?'

I struggled to give him an instant answer. I knew he was lying but I didn't know what his lies meant. As I stared at him, I saw doubt flicker across his brow, but he squashed it quickly and I did the same. 'I'm sure we can,' I supplied as an answer. 'It will take just a little bit of setting up. I'm glad we were able to get here ahead of them. Now, you're sure no one has been in here?'

'There's no sign of it,' he lied again.

I nodded though, already moving toward the door to leave. 'We need to prepare if we are going to try to catch the person perpetrating the break ins. You'll have to leave too, of course.'

If the suggestion came as a surprise to Vihaan, he showed no sign of it. He nodded his head once in acknowledgement, bowing it to look at the carpet. 'How long do you think this will take?' he asked, his head rising again to pierce me with his eyes. There was something behind them, something unreadable and untrustworthy.

'Impossible to say, sir,' replied Lieutenant Baker. 'I will assemble a team, but it would be prudent for you to stay out for the next few hours.' Baker glanced at me to see if that agreed with my thoughts. I nodded. 'Yes, a few hours at least. Do you have somewhere that you can stay in the meantime?'

'I think I will visit a bar. It has been quite the evening already.' His answer seemed to satisfy everyone, and he followed us from the room as Barbie led the way out. I paused to see which way he would head, then grabbed Barbie's arm to guide her the opposite way.

'What are you doing?' she asked when she saw me glancing back over my shoulder to check what he was doing.

I didn't answer straight away. I waited until Vihaan and Arabella turned a corner and disappeared from sight. Then, still holding Barbie's elbow, I wheeled her around and started heading back to his suite. 'He was lying.'

'About what?' Barbie asked.

As I fished in my handbag, I said, 'All of it.'

Lieutenant Baker overtook me to get to the door first. 'Hold on, Mrs Fisher. There was no calling card on his nightstand. I was first into the room. What is it that he was lying about?'

Jermaine answered for me. 'The carpet bore the four small indentations and the same line of dust as all the other rooms the calling card criminal has visited.' Baker's eyes went wide in realisation, then wider still when Jermaine added, 'That isn't the only lie he is telling.'

I swiped the door panel with my stolen universal keycard. Baker saw it and spluttered, shock stopping him from forming a coherent sentence. 'What? What, how?' I pushed open the door and went inside. 'Mrs Fisher, where did you get a universal door card?'

Rather than provide an answer, I said, 'That's not really a pertinent question to ask a lady.'

My answer confused him enough to make him pause, by which time I was across the room and staring at the indentations again. He caught up with me but if he wanted to quiz me about the door card I definitely shouldn't have, his line of questions were delayed by the sight in front of him.

Baker's voice came out as a hushed surprise, 'He lied.'

Barbie and Jermaine joined us. Barbie had a question for her butler friend. 'You said he was telling other lies.'

Jermaine sniffed and hung his head, clearly giving thought to what he wanted to say. 'Madam, you suggested earlier that were I to meet Rajesh I might be able to determine his sexuality because I have a nose for such things.' I held his gaze but didn't answer, questioning whether my words had been insulting or somehow bigoted. 'It's actually quite simple to observe if one knows what to look for. Vihaan is gay.' As I questioned why he was telling us that, Jermaine indicated around the room with his arm. In all of the posters, Vihaan had a girl on his arm, sometimes more than one.

'How can you tell?' Barbie wanted to know.

Jermaine glanced down at his pretty blonde friend. 'Your chest.'

'Huh?' she stared down at her boobs as did I and Baker. Baker realised what he was doing and looked away though as Barbie brought her eyes up to his and his cheeks coloured.

Jermaine explained. 'Heterosexual men notice your chest. They cannot help it. Even those with self-control, glance at it more often than they ought. Isn't that right, Lieutenant Baker?'

Lieutenant Baker had found a very interesting corner of the room to examine. 'Yeah, that sounds about right,' he mumbled.

Barbie shrugged. 'Boys stare at my boobs. I was aware of that.'

'Yet Vihaan didn't. Nor did he pay any attention to Arabella, another attractive woman wearing very little clothing. That he is hiding his sexuality might mean nothing. I suspect otherwise though.'

'And he lied about the calling card,' added Baker.

I had to correct him. 'We don't actually know that. What we believe is that the calling card criminal has been in here, but Vihaan might not have found the calling card himself.' The faces around me all said they doubted that was the case. I agreed with them. 'It feels unlikely, doesn't it? My point is; we don't know. So, for now, we have to proceed with the belief that he is probably lying but we don't know why.'

Baker moved toward the door. 'We should leave.' Then he fixed me with a hard stare. 'We also need to deal with the universal door card you have about your person, Mrs Fisher.'

Barbie tutted. 'I thought you wanted to be the cool hero in uniform and not the boring by the rules guy.' She stared him down, Jermaine and I falling in either side of her to join her withering stare.

Baker flapped his arms in defeat. 'I am going to get in so much trouble when this comes out,' he sighed.

Barbie giggled and rubbed her knuckles on his skull as she passed him, yelling, 'Boring,' as she darted out of the suite again.

Baker continued to mutter as he shut the door and made sure it was secure, then traipsed after us as we headed away. My head was filling with more clues and more conspiracy theories as the evening progressed. Despite my determination to work out who was responsible for murdering Dayita and my bragging challenge to Alistair that I would present the solution before him, I was getting nowhere, had an additional murder to contend with, and I was getting tired.

I wasn't even sure what my next move was or where we were heading. My feet were taking us back toward the front of the ship and my suite, but before we got there, we ran into Alistair's party coming the other way.

Trickster

Both parties came to a stop facing one another in the confined passageway. Devrani made and held eye contact with me but continued onwards, passing me as he continued to stare. Then he began to walk behind me and as I turned my own body to face him, it was like we were two prize fighters circling each other and looking for an opening.

'Can I help you?' I enquired. His behaviour was odd and felt rude. Were he not with Alistair I would simply continue onwards and ignore him.

He replied to my question though and stopped moving. 'I rather think we should help each other. We are both working towards the same end result, are we not? The successful capture of the murderer. Since we are both coming at this investigation from different angles, perhaps we are each learning different aspects. By sharing we can solve this more swiftly.' His attitude was still haughty but he was at least speaking to me as an equal now.

'Okay,' I conceded. 'What would you like to know?'

He glanced along the passageway in the direction we had come from. 'I am curious to learn what you were doing all the way back here?'

'That's easy,' I replied. 'We discovered a pattern to the room invasions. The calling card criminal is following a pattern. We hoped to be able to intercept him by predicting where he would strike next but we were too late. He had already been.'

Alistair stepped forward. 'Do you know where his next target will be?'

I gave him a sorry look. 'That's not so easy to determine. He is working in concentric circles, but his next target could be one of a dozen or more rooms as he has just completed a circle and will now start another.'

'Whose suite was it?' asked Devrani.

'Vihaan Veghale's.'

Devrani nodded as if my answer was in line with his expectations; an annoyingly knowing gesture of superior intellect. 'Are there any other facts which you have discovered which you can share at this time? We are all working toward the same goal,' he reminded me as if I was about to deny his request.

'I have reason to believe that Dayita may have been pregnant.' When his eyes lit up in question, I added, 'We found a pregnancy test in the waste receptacle in her room and one of the dancers, I don't know who, the person made sure I couldn't see their face, handed me a used test which showed a positive result.'

'Yes. Yes, that makes perfect sense.' Devrani smiled at himself as if he had just worked it all out.

'What makes sense?'

He didn't answer me though, he started walking again, onwards in the direction he had been heading when we met. 'No time to lose, dear captain. Our quarry is wiley but not infallible.'

'Hey,' I called at Devrani's back. 'I thought we were sharing.'

'You were sharing, foolish woman. Good luck with your investigation. You're barking up the wrong tree.' Then he was gone, turning a corner to vanish from sight.

Alistair shot me an embarrassed look as he went after him. 'I didn't know he was going to do that, Patricia. I am sorry.'

I waved him away. 'You should get after him, dear captain,' I repeated in a mocking tone. 'We shall see which of us is barking up the wrong tree soon enough.'

As Alistair bowed his head and slipped away, Bhukari, Schneider and the others following, Barbie came to stand next to me. 'He isn't very nice,' she commented.

'No,' I agreed. 'But despite playing the trickster, I think he is on the wrong trail and having told him about Dayita's pregnancy, I now wonder if I have misled him.'

Barbie eyed me curiously. 'How so?'

I started walking again as I tried to sort my thoughts into order. I was heading in the rough direction of my suite but my actual destination lay just beyond it. Jermaine and Lieutenant Baker fell into step behind us as I started to explain myself. 'I was handed the pregnancy test and that led us to visit Dayita's cabin. We found the room trashed so the assumption is that someone had been in there looking for something.'

'Hold on,' said Lieutenant Baker with a sigh. 'You were in her cabin?'

'Yes.'

'Earlier this evening?'

'Yes.'

'Should I ask how you gained entry?'

'No.' I waited to see if he had another question, decided that he didn't and pressed on. 'While we were there, we found an opal from Irani Patel's cufflinks.'

Baker gasped this time. 'You have evidence that places him in the murdered woman's room, and you haven't revealed it to anyone?'

It was my turn to sigh. I even tutted for good measure. 'It can't be used as evidence because there is no chain of evidence to demonstrate that it was ever in Dayita's room. We know it was and that is probably sufficient for our investigation, but the point is, it would be really damning if Irani hadn't admitted being there. If he denied it, we would know he was lying. As it is, he waved off his presence in her cabin as routine.'

Baker posed a good question. 'So who trashed Dayita's room and what were they looking for?'

'I think we might be able to work that out, but I want to look at what Irani was doing there if he wasn't having an affair with her.'

'You really think that's likely?' asked Barbie. 'If Dayita was pretending to be in a relationship with Rajesh, then it fits that if she were sleeping with Irani, Rajesh would know about it and Irani, having killed Dayita, would then need to silence Rajesh.'

I nodded my head. 'That's right. It does fit. It fits really nicely.'

'What about the calling cards though?' asked Jermaine. 'If Irani killed Dayita, why did he stick a calling card to her?'

Baker provided the answer. 'To throw people off the scent. He kept the card found in his suite earlier this evening then used it to confuse the investigation. I bet he doesn't have the card anymore.'

'We should ask him right now,' said Barbie, quickening her pace as excitement took over.

Baker slowed his pace though as he thought of something. 'Where did he get a second one to shove into Rajesh's mouth when he killed him?'

We all stopped to consider that question and I circled back to my original thoughts on the case. 'I still don't think Irani is the killer.'

'Why not, madam?' asked Jermaine, sounding politely curious rather than directly suggesting I was wrong or perhaps bonkers.

I still didn't have an answer though. 'It doesn't smell right?' I tried, kind of shrugging as I said it. 'When Irani jumped in to protect Dayita from Taginda earlier, did any of you get the sense that the two of them were lovers?'

'I wasn't there, madam.'

'Neither was I,' added Baker.

I looked at Barbie. 'Nor me,' she shrugged.

'Okay, well that doesn't help. They didn't, you're just going to have to take my word for it.'

'How would you describe them then?' asked Baker.

Again, with the good questions. I had to think about it, but I knew the answer. 'Fatherly. He came across as fatherly, which is not how I have seen him with anyone else.' Having said the word and articulated my thoughts, a piece of the puzzle dropped into place. I quickened my pace. 'We need to get back to my suite and we need to speak to Mrs Patel.'

Barbie skipped along next to me, excited by my sudden sense of purpose. 'Ooh, what we are we going to do?'

'Research,' I said, gritted determination in my voice.

'Oh,' replied Barbie doing nothing to hide her disappointment. 'That doesn't sound very exciting.'

'It will be,' I assured her and started to jog.

Research

'What is it we are looking for?' asked Barbie as she poised her fingers over the keyboard.

'Irani Patel. See what you can find out about his children, his ex-wives, if he has any, his movie career. I can't help remembering Shane and Tarquin and wondering how much pain we could have saved ourselves if we had just done more research at the start.' No one argued with me, least of all Jermaine, who had suffered a blow to the head that night which could have been far worse than it was.

I left Barbie to see what she could find as I took my shoes off again. I really wanted to shuck my dress completely, and then questioned why I couldn't. The after party was done with; I didn't need to be in a ball gown again tonight. The results show tomorrow might not even take place at the rate the show was going so I wouldn't need it then either.

Anna followed me to my bedroom where I spotted the ruined dress with the paint on it. I had all but forgotten about it. I crossed the room to where it was now pointlessly hung back on a hanger. I didn't think it could be salvaged so it was good for the trash bin and little else. Where had the paint come from though? When Jermaine pointed it out, I just assumed I had leaned on something but where would I find yellow paint? Nothing on the ship was painted yellow.

'Paint,' I said the word out loud and got a question in response from Jermaine when he appeared at my door a few seconds later.

'Did you call me, madam?'

Skewing my lips to one side as I thought, I looked up at him. 'I did not.' I was holding the dress to show him the paint. 'Where did this come from?'

'I couldn't say, madam.'

'Paint,' I said the word again. Then I let the dress go and took my phone from my handbag. Rick answered almost straight away.

'Patricia, so wonderful to hear your voice. Do you have another wild goose chase for us two poor smucks to embark upon?' I heard Akamu's voice in the background, his deep bass rumble sounding just as negative as Rick's.

'I take it you have had no luck so far then?'

'No,' he replied mockingly. 'Honestly, Patricia, we need a little more to go on.'

'Well, then it's a good thing I called, isn't it? I think you need to look at paint.'

'Paint?' Rick repeated.

'Yes, paint.'

'Paint,' he repeated again.

I was beginning to feel like we were stuck on a loop. 'Specifically, oil paintings.'

Rick was silent for a second and it was as if I could hear his gears turning. 'That might hold some merit, you know?' In the background I heard him relay my thoughts to Akamu before he came back onto the phone. 'Okay, I think we know someone who might know someone. Give us a while, okay?'

We disconnected and I tapped my phone to my chin in thought still. Jermaine, patient as always, waited for me to be ready to speak. I forgot all about changing out of my ball gown though as I crossed the room back toward the door once more. Jermaine spun about and led the way back into the living area where he stood to one side so I could pass.

I walked over to the safe and the oil painting there, opened it where it hinged from the right and studied it. I looked at the hinges and I looked at the frame. I am far from being an art expert, so I wasn't looking with an educated eye, but I saw what I thought I might see and now I needed to check it against another.

I pushed the frame back into place, covering the safe again. 'Lieutenant Baker, can you assist me, please?'

'Err, sure,' he said, standing up. He had been looking over Barbie's shoulder at the computer screen as the two of them dug into Irani's past. 'What are we doing?'

'We need to visit the suite next door.' He held up both hands, each one pointing in a different direction because there were, of course, suites either side of me. I pointed to the front of the ship. 'Mr Patel in the Montgomery Suite. If he is there, I have some questions for him. If not, I need you to let me in so I can look at something.'

'Don't you want to see what we turn up first?' asked Barbie, swivelling in her chair to face me.

I shook my head. 'No time.'

Mrs Patel

As it turned out, Irani Patel wasn't there, but his wife answered the door, the small mousy woman still staring at the deck as she spoke to us. 'I'm afraid my husband is not here. You'll have to come back later,' she murmured, her voice barely audible.

'No, it's you I want to see, Mrs Patel,' I replied, my tone breezy and light as if I was really pleased to see her. Her head snapped up and I thought perhaps it was the first time I had actually seen her face.

Surprised that it was her I wanted to see, Mrs Patel took a step back from the doorway she had been blocking and, seeing my chance, I went inside without her inviting me to do so. 'Thank you so much for giving me a little of your time. We won't keep you long I promise.'

She closed the door behind Baker as he too came in to stand next to me, but she wasn't happy about it. 'Oh. Oh, I don't know. I don't like to talk to people without Irani present.'

'Oh, come now,' I encouraged her. 'There's nothing to be afraid of. You and I are just two mature women having a chat.'

'What is it you want to chat about?' she asked. Her head and eyes were cast back down at the carpet again and she hadn't moved away from the door as if staying close to the edge of the cabin afforded her some safety.

She had invited me to pose a question though, so I did. 'I was curious about why you provided a false alibi for Irani earlier?'

Her head snapped up again, her mouth open and her cheeks glowing at my accusation. 'I did no such thing. I told the truth.'

'That right before the show, you were overcome by passion for your husband and the two of you were having sex?'

'Yes, that's right.'

'No, it isn't,' I insisted. I felt bad that I was calling her a liar, but she was lying, and I wanted to know why. 'Did Irani kill Dayita? Are you covering for him?'

'No!' she shouted her answer. 'I want you to leave now.' Her demand was a reasonable one and I didn't know where we stood legally speaking. I had Lieutenant Baker with me and on the ocean the laws about what you can and cannot do in the pursuit of justice are very different to those on land, I wasn't sure we could impose ourselves on her like this though when we had very little justifiable cause.

She pointed to the door, her eyes up and blazing hatred at me as I failed to move. So I did move. I just didn't go the way she was pointing. I caught Baker by surprise as well when I set off toward the centre of the living area and the oil painting that covered the safe. Her suite was arranged much the same as mine, so it was easy to navigate.

She cried out, 'Hey,' as I defied her and raced after me. She wasn't fast enough and I had the oil painting swung away from the safe by the time she got to me. I only needed a second to confirm what I hoped to see was there and stepped away again before she could snatch the painting from my hands. 'You have no right to be in here prying. Please leave.'

'We really should go, Mrs Fisher,' Baker added, gesturing with his hand that I should head toward the door before I caused a problem.

'My husband will hear of this,' Mrs Patel threatened as I walked calmly back toward the door.

Over my shoulder I replied. 'Your husband is going to be accused of murder and I am the one that will prove he isn't guilty, Mrs Patel. You should be helping me.'

'No! No help,' she raged. Perhaps my approach had been too aggressive. Perhaps I should have introduced the idea that she was lying about the alibi after I won her trust. Too late now, but as we got near to the small lobby by the door, we passed a bathroom and I spotted something.

With the other two following me, neither could do anything when I darted inside the toilet and shut the door. Outside, Mrs Patel complained bitterly about the awful woman that wouldn't leave her alone and Lieutenant Baker did his best to placate her and assure her we would be leaving just as soon as I came back out from the locked toilet.

The thing I had spotted was a packet of tablets. They looked to be prescription drugs with a pharmacy label stuck to the outside rather than over the counter drugs one might buy in a store. They were exactly that, and the label told me everything I wanted to know about them: they were prescribed to Irani Patel and were to be taken for anxiety.

I checked inside the box as Mrs Patel hammered on the toilet door. The blister pack was almost empty, just one tablet remained which meant Irani had worked his way through the rest of them. I popped the packet into my handbag, flushed the toilet to suggest that I had rushed into her bathroom for a call of nature and undid the lock.

Mrs Patel's face was flushed and angry. 'I'm terribly sorry, Mrs Patel. I became ever so queasy. It has passed now.' She had no reply for me, just a stony stare, but she let me pass and I made my way to the door. Lieutenant Baker did his best to keep his body between the two of us, not that I thought it necessary, but the door slammed hard after he joined me in the passageway in what seemed like an uncharacteristic display of emotion from the small Indian woman.

Now alone in the passageway, Baker raised his eyebrows at me. 'What was all that about, Mrs Fisher?'

I showed him the packet. 'The puzzle is coming together.'

My cryptic reply did nothing to answer his question and he spluttered as I started back to my suite, leaving him standing in the passage by himself. 'You just took someone's prescription medicine? We have to give that back.'

'No, it's a clue.'

'That doesn't matter,' he countered.

'Catching the killer does.' I could sense that he was unhappy, so I stopped and met his eyes. We were right outside the door to my suite, but I held off swiping my keycard. I held up the packet again. 'There is only one tablet left in this packet and they are not life-saving drugs that a person might take for a heart condition. They are Irani Patel's and he uses them to deal with anxiety, the sort of condition which might manifest as a panic attack.'

I let the words sink in and gave the security officer a moment to connect the dots. His eyes, which had been unfocused as he worked the new information around in his head, came back to look at mine when he saw what it meant. Then he nodded and fell in place to my side so I could open the door.

The Patels

Jermaine and Barbie looked up as we came in. 'You won't believe what we found out,' announced Barbie. Anna jumped off the couch to greet me, pleased to see me every time I went out the door and came back in. Baker froze in case she planned to ravage his ankles again, but she had grown used to him now, no longer seeing him as a threat. She trotted after me as I kicked my shoes off and went into the living area.

'You think that Dayita is Irani Patel's daughter,' I replied.

Both of the them stared at me. 'Madam how could you have possibly guessed that?' asked Jermaine.

'Yeah,' added Barbie. 'That's some next level voodoo you are doing there, Patty.'

I smiled back at them, showing my teeth in a big cheeky grin. 'I said it earlier actually. I said he looked more fatherly than anything else and then it hit me. That was why he was trying to be protective of her and why he was going to her room. He told the lie about visiting the rooms of other people from the show and soon got called out, but he had a reason to visit Dayita. I don't think he has known for very long though and I don't think his wife knows at all.'

'Why do you say that?' asked Baker.

Instead of answering, I posed a question myself, 'How long have they been married?'

Barbie glanced down at her notes. 'Um, thirty-three years.'

'And how old was Dayita?'

She already knew the answer to that one. 'Twenty-six.' I had thought she was younger even than that, but the math told the same story regardless; if Dayita was Irani's daughter, then he she came from an affair that he most likely still didn't want his wife to know about.

'So what else did you find?' I asked as I moved across the room to join them at the computer.

Barbie turned back to the screen. 'Where to start? We went back to the start of Irani's career. He was successful very early on, leaving acting school in Mumbai and landing a lead role weeks later. The roles just flowed after that, film after film for years, his handsome face and flawless smile winning him a large following. There are a lot of articles about his ability as an actor, he won several awards in Bollywood.'

'There are articles about his private life too,' Jermaine took up the narrative. 'His wife, Sheba, was also a film actor and well known by the Indian public, had a very public pregnancy not long after they were married. Irani and Sheba were a celebrity couple, the darlings of the Indian press it would seem, getting the same sort of attention in their homeland that a Hollywood couple might get in America.'

'They lost the baby though, didn't they?' I asked, already certain I knew the answer.

Jermaine offered me a sad nod. 'Again, it was very public. The baby died during labour due to complications in the birth. None of the articles we found elaborated on what the difficulties were but the details seem unimportant. After that the press followed them even more closely, public sympathy for the couple and especially Mrs Patel was highly vocal, but I think it drove her away from the limelight, causing her to become a recluse almost.'

It was Barbie's turn to continue the story. 'She then miscarried several times and vanished from public life. There are very few mentions of her after that, until Irani landed the role of show host for *Stars that Dance* a few years ago. Then she gets some by-lines and a few brief references to her stuttering film career, but the interesting article that made us look at Dayita was just a couple of years after the last miscarriage. Sheba was no longer a public figure and wasn't working but Irani was linked to a female costar during filming one of his most successful movies. It was in Costa Rica and the actress's name is Amba Ahuya.' Barbie pushed back her chair and swivelled to face the rest of us. 'So far there's nothing here to get excited about, but Irani is famous for something he probably doesn't care for.' She let the announcement hang tantalising for a moment before filling in the blank. 'He has a third nipple.'

Suddenly we had a tangible if not conclusive link. Irani has an affair with a costar, she has a baby but never tells him about it and they never see each other again. Amba either hides her daughter's parentage from Dayita or lied about it, or perhaps Dayita always knew the truth but never spoke of it. Whatever the case, I was willing to bet that the truth had recently come to the attention of Irani Patel. Did that mean he hadn't killed her though?

Lieutenant Baker had the same thought. 'If Irani Patel recently found out that he has an adult daughter that proves an infidelity, he might have wanted to silence her. Would he feel any bond to Dayita as a daughter if he had never known her?'

'Hard to say,' I admitted. 'I think he did though. We still need to consider that she was pregnant.' Three sets of eyes looked at me. 'She was pregnant, so she was having Irani's grandchild. For a man that thought he had no children and had very publicly remained childless, this might have been a lifeline he never imagined.'

'Only he can answer that,' said Jermaine, hitting the nail on the head.

'We need to talk to him.' I started back toward the door again, Anna leaping off the couch hopeful and excited that we were going out again. 'I need to ask him about the anxiety as well.' Then I took a moment to explain to Barbie and Jermaine about the drugs.

While Jermaine fetched Anna's lead, I grimaced at my shoes, argued internally about indulging my desire to get changed and berated myself for being weak. Then put the damned shoes on again anyway.

This would all be over soon I suspected, and then I could get into bed in my pyjamas and not care two hoots about footwear. I was wrong though; this wasn't about to be over and I wasn't going to get to speak to Irani any time soon.

In Custody

We could hear a commotion as soon as we opened the door to my suite. Anna's ears pricked up and she barked at the noise, tilting her head to one side as she tried to work out what she could hear. It was coming from the direction of the elevators, just around the corner where the passageway passing my suite ended in an atrium from which the rest of the ship could be accessed.

Anna dragged me along, her shoulders hunched as she put as much effort in as she could to propel herself forward. Jermaine, Barbie and Lieutenant Baker all followed behind me as I tried to control the unruly dog.

Before I got to the corner, I could tell who I was listening to: it was the show's female producer, the woman with the severe hair and severe glasses. She was locked in an argument over something or someone and the person on the other end of her temper was Devrani Bharma.

'It doesn't matter that you have a show scheduled for tomorrow evening. The host is not going to be available for it,' he said calmly.

The woman screamed something back at him which I couldn't understand due to her thick accent but I suspected it would be bleeped out if it was shown on television. 'How am I supposed to manage that?' she demanded.'

'Deepika.' I finally learned her name. 'Deepika,' Devrani said with a sigh. 'Irani has been taken into custody and will be charged with two counts of murder. You are not the first producer in the history of television to be thrown a curveball. If he dropped dead of a heart attack you would be faced with the same problem. It is not insurmountable, and we will work with you to find a suitable replacement from those persons available.'

'I'll do it.' I turned the corner to find a crowd gathered in front of the elevators. Alistair was among them though there were no other white uniforms visible. Most likely they were with Irani if indeed he had been taken into custody. The volunteer to be the new host was Taginda, her opportunistic grasp for power no surprise to anyone present. When Devrani, Deepika and others turned her way, she said, 'What? You need someone, my dance partner is dead, and I am the most popular person on the show.'

Deepika's shoulders slumped. 'She might have a point.'

I didn't care about the show, it was entirely unimportant. I wanted to make sure we had the right man though and I wasn't sure Devrani had his facts straight. I interrupted before anyone else could speak. 'What makes you think that Irani killed his daughter?'

All eyes swung my way. The question was deliberately inflammatory; I was betting they had no idea about the link between Dayita and Irani and I knew it would get their attention. Devrani had a question but Alistair got there first. 'What do you mean, Patricia? Who is his daughter?'

'Dayita is... was. Hadn't you worked that bit out yet?'

Devrani chose that moment to laugh. 'What utter nonsense. Next you'll tell us that he wasn't sleeping with the girl.'

'He wasn't.'

'And that the baby she carried wasn't his.'

'It isn't.'

'What else? The murderer is the same person that has been leaving the calling card for the last two weeks and that person just decided to change their tactic from breaking into rooms, to murdering random television personalities.'

'Yes.'

Alistair stared at me. 'Really?'

I sighed. He was a lovely man, but he wasn't much of a detective. 'No, Alistair. Not really. How much research did you do, Mr Bharma? Or did you just rely on your sense of intuition? Irani Patel fathered Dayita with Amba Ahuya, an actress he co-starred with many years ago. I haven't spoken to him about it yet, that's where we were heading actually, but I don't think he knew about Dayita until recently. Maybe she didn't know either, but the point is they share a rare genetic anomaly that is generally passed on through birth. She is his daughter and the baby she carried was his grandchild. He was keeping it quiet because he was married to Sheba at the time of his infidelity.'

'You can prove any of this?' Devrani asked, his tone mocking and a smile on his face as it were amusingly fanciful. I found myself wanting to slap his head once or maybe ten times.

'I doubt that I need to, Devrani. You already have Irani in custody I understand.'

Alistair bowed his head, sensing that he might have been misguided. 'Yes.'

'Then perhaps you should ask him about Dayita. If he knows that the secret is out, I doubt he will continue to deny it.'

Devrani wasn't about to be defeated though. He clearly thought he had a winning theory. 'Why then, did his wife provide a false alibi? Why did the calling card from Irani's pocket end up stuck to Dayita's body?' He took a step toward me, his cool exterior beginning to crack with the constant questioning. Anna took a dislike to his advancing foot though and snapped at it, causing him to jerk back out of her way.

It stopped him from asking questions so I could pose one of my own. 'Do you know why Irani looked so sweaty and uncomfortable when he arrived only just in time to open the show?' As soon as the words left my mouth, I realised my mistake.

Devrani smiled down at me. 'Because he had just been busy murdering Dayita. Even someone as cold and cunning as Irani would work up a sweat plunging a knife through a young woman's chest.'

'What if she is his daughter?' Alistair asked.

The annoying television detective had an answer for that too though. 'Then he murdered her to keep the secret. He is the patriarch of Indian public culture. Everyone loves him. What would a scandal like this do to his popularity? And would he kill to protect his image? I think he would, and he did, and he will lie to protect himself now.'

'I can see that he is going to have trouble convincing you of his innocence, so I guess I'll have to do it for him. Are you not curious about what happened to Rajesh or do you think that Irani killed him as well?'

I got the amused smile from him again, like he was the wise teacher and I the hopeful student trying to impress him but falling well short of the mark. 'You think there is more than one murderer here?' Alistair looked at me curiously as well. I thought about telling them everything. I thought about telling them why they were wrong, but I didn't have all the pieces yet. It would work better if I let Devrani think he had the upper hand because then I could crush him later.

Deepika wanted to know more though. 'So which is it? Is Irani Dayita's father? Did he kill her? Who killed Rajesh? Can I have my host back for the results show tomorrow?'

Taginda wanted to voice her thoughts too. 'You don't need him, Deepika. He's been hogging the limelight for too long and just think what will happen when the scandal comes out to ruin him. You should get some distance between him and the show now so you are protected.'

I wanted to talk to Irani, I had a stack of questions for him, but I thought that I already knew the answer to most of them. The things I didn't know or couldn't yet work out were not to do with him. They were to do with the other things that were going on. I hadn't worked out who had killed Dayita and Rajesh, I was just certain that Irani hadn't despite the evidence stacking up against him.

But if I couldn't talk to Irani, what was my next move? Barbie, Jermaine and Lieutenant Baker were all hovering just behind me, waiting for me to make a decision. I turned to them, changed my mind and turned back to Deepika. 'You should plan to have Irani hosting the show tomorrow. I think we can get this cleared up by then.'

'Really?' she called after me, but I was already walking away. 'So who did kill Dayita then?'

I ignored her and kept on walking. Alistair's voice stopped me though. He had run to catch up with me. 'Do you really think Devrani has it wrong? The case against Irani is overwhelming.'

'Because we know he had one of the calling cards, a relatively rare commodity and then couldn't find it when one was found impaled on a dead woman he is suspected of having an affair with?'

'Can you prove that she is his daughter?' he demanded.

'Why don't you ask him?' I snapped my reply and it felt like we were having a fight.

Alistair pursed his lips and nodded. Then calmly, he said, 'I think I will do that. Proving she is his daughter doesn't prove he didn't kill her though. His unexplained whereabouts prior to the show which coincides with when she was murdered, he arrives sweaty and looking pale and we know it cannot have been anyone else from among the stars and dancers because they were all visible. If not him, then who? And why?'

I took his hand. I wanted us to be alright but somehow we had ended up on opposing sides. I needed to get this night done, find the evidence that would show us all who the killer was and get back to where we were this afternoon; basking in the glow of new relationship bliss. 'I will show you everything as soon as I have it. You don't have to trust me.' He pulled a face, but I stopped him from arguing by continuing to talk. 'It's okay, and you don't have to release Irani Patel, not yet anyway. I would make sure that he is well treated though because you will be letting him go in a few hours.'

'You're sure?' he asked.

Instead of answering his redundant question, I said, 'I have work to do. I'll call you when I am ready.' Then I left him, indicating with my eyes that my friends should all come with me as I headed back toward my suite.

'Where are we going?' hissed Barbie.

What It is All About

The answer to her question was back to my suite to quickly regroup. I needed to talk to Rick and Akamu again, to see how they were getting on and get them to work quicker if possible. I didn't know if they would even be able to find the information I needed but we were running out of time either way. I also needed Barbie and Jermaine to get back on the computer, there was more research I needed them to do. Finally, I needed something to eat. I had been surviving on nibbles all evening and needed someone to hand me a fat sandwich with a side of fries. It was late and I wanted dirty food to keep me going.

Yet again, I kicked my shoes off and promised myself I would find better footwear before I went out again. Anna charged across the room to the kitchen where her water bowl sat waiting. I could hear her thirstily lapping at it by the time I got into the living space.

On the way to my suite, I explained my thoughts and needs so Jermaine was already in the kitchen by the time Barbie sat at the computer. Jermaine would produce a first-class feast from raw ingredients in no time at all and somehow make it as satisfying as late-night fast food while also ensuring it was flavourful and probably nutritious.

The noise of a chopping blade reassured me as I took out my phone to call Rick again. This time it was Akamu that answered though. 'Hey, Patricia, how's the murder enquiry going?'

I wrinkled my nose as I thought about what answer I could give. 'I don't know,' I tried. 'I mean, I think I know who didn't do it, which is the guy they have fingered for it already and who looks guilty as all hell, but I don't know who did do it. Yet.'

'Uh-huh? So are you calling to see what us two geniuses have found?'

'Have you found something?' The timbre of his voice when he bragged about being a genius filled me with hope that he was.

He sighed though. 'We think so. It's... It's. Look it will be easier to show you, I think. Can you come to our cabin?'

'Sure. Now?'

'If that works for you. Rick went to get some beer; he says he thinks better when he is relaxed.' I understood what he meant, my brain worked far better with a gin and tonic to fuel it. 'We have to make another call shortly. We got the guy's daughter earlier. She said he was taking a nap and we should call back in a while. I guess he's kind of old.'

'Okay. I'll be down in a little while.' I wanted to eat first but when I glanced across at the kitchen, I knew it was going to be twenty minutes or more before Jermaine served supper, so I changed my mind. 'Better yet, I'm coming now. See you in a few minutes.'

It wouldn't take long to get to their cabin, it was on the eighteenth deck on the starboard side and not far from where the elevators nearest to me opened up. If I didn't have to wait for the elevators, it would take about two minutes to get there. I stared at the lobby and the high-heeled, expensive and uncomfortable shoes waiting for me there and swore at myself. I could go and find other shoes, but time was already ticking away.

'I'm going to see Rick and Akamu,' I announced, then whistled for Anna to join me. I might as well take her outside to do her thing before bed on my way there.

Jermaine put down the saucepan he was holding and pulled off his apron. 'I'll accompany you, madam.'

'No, you won't. You get back in that kitchen and make me some food,' I teased. 'Lieutenant Baker can manage to keep me safe for a few minutes.'

Hearing his name, the young security officer looked up. He was sitting on the couch and looking weary; it had probably been a long day for him already, but he got back on his feet and gave Jermaine a thumbs up on his way to the door.

I doubted I had any need for a personal armed security escort, but given my history on this ship, I knew Jermaine would be happier knowing I had one. Nothing happened, of course. The elevator was empty, and we reached Rick and Akamu's cabin in under three minutes. I got there so fast, in fact, that I wondered if I would beat Rick back from his beer run.

I hadn't though, he answered the door with a bottle of Corona in his hand, condensation on it telling me it was fresh and cold. He saw me eyeing it as he took a swig and backed away from the door to let me in. 'You want one?' he asked. 'We have plenty.' Anna let herself in, sniffing Rick's feet and heading to look for Akamu because she knew he was a sucker for small dogs and would make a fuss of her.

I took the offered beer gratefully, but Lieutenant Baker declined, pointing to the side arm he carried. Rick nodded that he agreed with the policy. The beer was cold and refreshing but I wanted to know what they had found.

So did Lieutenant Baker, who had no idea what they were even up to. 'Do you want to explain?' asked Rick. 'This is your hair-brained plan after all.'

I tipped my beer at him in mock salute. 'I got the idea that the calling card criminal must be known somewhere. It is such a unique thing to do; leaving a calling card to brag that you were there, that I figured if the criminal had ever operated before, there must be a record of it somewhere.'

'That makes sense,' Baker conceded.

'He or she, or maybe even they, are breaking into people's cabins and doing something that requires a small table or a piece of equipment that leaves four small footprints in the carpet. The fact that it leaves footprints means it must be heavy and that confused me for a while. I just couldn't work out what they were doing.'

'What are they doing?' he asked.

I took another swig of beer. 'I'm getting there. With these two old sheriffs to call upon I figured that between them they must have quite a network of old cops, old guys from other law enforcement agencies, people that know people and so on that they could tap into. If there had ever been a criminal leaving a calling card then someone somewhere would know about it.'

'That was the task she set us anyway,' said Akamu. Then he did a terrible rendition of my voice, making his high and squeaky and putting on a rubbish English accent. 'Guys, I want you to find some crazy criminal that may or may not have employed the same tactic at some point in the past. By the way, I don't know which country that might have been in, what decade or if the person was ever caught.'

'Easy,' laughed Rick, not meaning a word of it.

'But you have found something, haven't you?' I pointed out, choosing not to point out that Akamu's version of my voice made me sound like the queen, if the queen sounded like a bad drag act.

'So what did you find?' asked Baker, sitting forward in his chair and getting carried away with the mystery of it.

Rick frowned deeply, his bushy eyebrows forming one where they met in the middle. 'Nothing, initially.'

'There was just too much territory to cover,' added Akamu, taking a draught of his own beer.

While his friend slaked his thirst, Rick took over. 'Until Patricia threw us a bone and said it might have something to do with oil paintings.'

Lieutenant Baker swung his gaze to look at me. 'I spotted that the small table or whatever it is, is always in more or less the same place in each of the suites; right in front of the safe. To start with I thought the criminal must be breaking into the safes and stealing something, but the reports are adamant that nothing has been taken.'

'That's right,' Baker agreed.

'Looking at the safe in my suite and scratching my head because I couldn't make sense of it, I had to ask what could be taken that no one would ever notice.'

Baker stared at me, waiting for me to tell him, but broke first and said, 'I give up. I have no idea.'

'An oil painting,' I supplied.

He frowned at me. 'Everyone would notice if an oil painting was taken. And they weren't taken. All the oil paintings and ornaments and everything else in every suite was checked and accounted for. I oversaw several of the inventories myself.'

I grinned a deep grin and shot him down in flames. 'What if the original, priceless, masterpiece of an oil painting was replaced by a forgery?' I watched the colour drain from his cheeks. 'The table, or whatever it is, is used to support the oil painting while the thief is working on it. I noticed that the heads of the brass screws holding the hinges in place had fresh marks on them; someone had unscrewed them recently. Not only that, in each suite where we found the indentation, we also found a line of dust. The cleaners do an amazing job of keeping the ship clean, no doubt giving extra care to the best suites. They don't clean inside the oil painting that covers the safe though. Maybe they don't even know it hinges out, but over the weeks, months and years, a layer of dust had built up on the bottom ledge of the frame on the inside. Taking it off and turning it over dislodges it.'

Baker slumped back into his chair. He saw the simple truth of it. 'So, this is all about stealing the Aurelia's art collection?'

'What's it worth, kid?' asked Rick. 'I know nothing about art, but I know people pay way too much for it and there have been a stack of unsolved art thefts over the years. Some rich collector wants the original and doesn't care how he comes by it; boom, you've got yourself a crime.'

Baker sat forward again. 'So, who's the thief? Who is leaving the calling cards?'

'That's what we are trying to find out.' I put the empty beer bottle down meaningfully as I stood up. 'You said you have someone to call?'

Rick looked at his watch then glanced at Akamu. 'You think we have given them long enough?'

Akamu looked at the clock, shrugged and picked up the phone. He dialled a number, squinting at a piece of paper on the desk as he did, then put the phone on speaker for everyone to hear.

It started ringing and a woman's voice came onto the phone. 'Hello.'

'Hello again,' Akamu answered. 'This is retired Police Lieutenant Akamu Kameāloha. We spoke earlier, I was hoping to speak to your father, is he awake now?'

I worried that the woman would tell me he was still asleep or that he wasn't available, but I needn't have been concerned. I could hear another voice in the background, an old but strong man's voice and he was fighting to get to the phone.

'Is that them?' We all heard him say. The woman said something I couldn't quite catch but which sounded like a warning to not overdo it or get excited, but the next thing we heard was the man's voice booming through the phone line. 'Hello. This is retired Deputy Commissioner Frank Tremblay of the Montreal Police department. I understand you want to talk to me about an old case.'

The man had a wonderful French twang to his voice, but I knew Montreal to have the second largest French speaking population outside of Paris; it was amazing what one learned when one left the house and got out into the world.

Akamu leaned toward the phone and licked his lips. 'That's right, sir. We don't know each other. I had to make a lot of calls to track down someone who might know what I am talking about...'

'That's okay, sonny,' the old man replied, cutting in over the top of Akamu. 'There's no need for all the preamble. I got a call from one of my old sergeants. He told me there was someone asking questions about old Frederick the Forger and he knew I would want to talk to you.'

'Frederick the Forger?' I asked, my voice cutting through the quiet as the retired deputy commissioner stopped talking.

He started again though. 'It seems I have an audience. Who else is there?'

'Sorry. I'm Patricia Fisher. I also have another retired police officer from Hawaii with me, Rick Hutton and Lieutenant Baker, he's part of the security on board the Aurelia.'

'The Aurelia? What's an Aurelia?'

Rick leaned forward to speak. 'It's a cruise ship, sir. We are on board a cruise ship somewhere off the coast of India. The art thefts, if that is what is happening, are all occurring in the suites on the upper deck.'

The old man at the other end laughed. 'That sounds like my Freddy. I thought he'd be dead by now. The man must be in his nineties, maybe older. We never caught him; you see. He was elusive and he was clever. Too clever maybe because he left such a trail. Everywhere he went, he left a calling card in the house. Back then he was targeting millionaires. People joked that you knew you were rich enough when Freddy stole from you. It was a pride thing, I think. He was so good at forging and breaking in and stealing the art that no one would have ever known he had been there if he hadn't left the cards. He wants to sell stolen art but how do you claim you have the original if it hasn't been reported stolen? He wanted everyone to know how good he was. He even stole from art galleries and museums. The man was a genius.'

'You sound like you admire him,' I commented.

The old man chuckled again. 'Well, I guess I do. To be that good, to evade us all that time, he was a rare talent. I only came close once. He created patterns; you see. In 1963 I was still a young detective, but I had been handed this case a couple of years beforehand and I had no idea what to do with it. Everyone else that had tried to work out how to catch the guy had got nowhere but I saw a pattern to his thefts. It was always on the same day. That was one thing. Always on a Thursday. I couldn't work out why, still haven't actually. Then, when I looked a little closer, I could see a pattern to the geography as well. The richest zip code in Montreal is Summit Park and Summit Park is a purpose-built area with roads that intersect at right angles. Like New York and a few other places, it is basically a big grid. Well, old Freddy was working a pattern there and I managed to get ahead of him. He wasn't going after any old house, of course. I had to canvass the area to find out who had expensive artwork worth stealing. It was a surprisingly small number.'

'What happened?' my question came out as a whisper; I was mesmerized by the story.

Yet again the old man chuckled. 'We set a trap for him in the house I was certain he was going to hit next, but something tipped him off. I staked out that house for two weeks with my chief breathing down my neck for wasting my time and everyone else's. They pulled the plug on the case, said it had gone cold. You know what happened? He stole the damn painting the night after we left the house.' He chuckled again. 'That's when I almost caught him.'

The old man was weaving the tale so well I almost felt my breath catch when he talked about catching the forger. I bit my lip so I wouldn't speak and listened for the rest of the story.

'I just had this feeling he would, you know. The chief wanted to put me onto another assignment, but I had some holiday time accrued so I took that. I genuinely planned to spend the time with my wife, but I couldn't shake the feeling that he was going to steal that painting. She sure was mad when I went out that night.' He chuckled again remembering it. 'He was there, just as I knew he would be. That's the only time I drew my weapon in a forty-six-year career.' His voice took on a faraway tone, no doubt picturing it all in his head as he retold the story and I pictured him at the other end of the phone with his eyes closed; a young man again and pursuing a thief. 'I waited for him to come out of the house and I shouted for him to stop. Do you know what he said? In the dark, with my gun aimed at him, he said, "Well done." Then he threw the painting at me and ran.'

The old man fell silent and I thought that was the end of his tale for a moment. Around the desk, all four of us were being drawn forward by his silence, each of us wanting to know how the forger just got away. 'I let him go,' the old man finally admitted. 'I could have shot him, I had a clean shot, just for a second before he went over the fence. I hesitated though, something about killing him just seemed wrong. I've… I've never told anyone that before.' He sounded relieved by his admission as if a great weight had finally been unburdened.

To fill the silence, I said, 'Well, I think he is on board this ship with us right now.'

The old man chuckled again. 'Good luck catching him. This guy is smoke. I followed his activities for years. I would get a whiff of a crime in France or in Spain or Mexico and I was sure it was him. Sure enough, when I did a little digging, someone would report that a calling card was found where the artwork was taken and a clever forgery would be found in its place. Half the time it took an expert to tell the difference, but I understand they can do it easily now with some kind of scope that determines how old the paint is.'

'Do you have any advice?' Rick asked.

'Hold on a moment, sonny. That's not the end of my story. There's more yet.' What more could there be? 'About a month after he got away from me that night, I woke in the morning to find a calling card on my nightstand. Freddy had broken into my house that night and left it there while I was sleeping.' This time my breath really did catch in my throat. 'I leapt out of bed and found my gun, but he hadn't meant me any harm. On the back of the card was a note. It read, "No one else has even come close." But that's not the best part.'

'Oh, my. What is?' I blurted.

'Downstairs in our kitchen was a painting. It was in one of the tubes he uses to transport the rolled canvasses. I swear I could barely control my fingers as I rolled it out, but there, on my dining room table, was a priceless Rembrandt.'

'What did you do with it?'

Yet again the old man chuckled. 'That, my dear lady, is a story for another day. Rick?'

'Sir?'

'You asked for my advice?'

'That I did, sir?'

'Well here it is. Give up. He'll be caught only if he wants to be.' The words surprised me; I had expected him to tell us to go get him. The old man wasn't finished though. 'However, if you've got some gumption in your boots and feel up to the challenge, watch for his patterns. I spotted one in Montreal and I have seen them in his work since. Never soon enough to do anything about it but the patterns were always there. If he is on board that ship with you, he is most likely stealing things in a pattern. I can't tell you why. Maybe he is autistic like that *Rainman* film and just sees numbers. Maybe it's something else, like why he always stole on a Thursday back then. If you catch him, you ask him for me, okay?'

I nodded my head, my silent reply unheard by the old man in Canada. 'I promise to do that,' I added so he could hear.

'Okay then. I think that's about it, folks. Unless you have any more questions, I think I had better get off the phone and let you get on with laying a trap.'

We all thanked him for his time and for his advice. Then Akamu hung up the handset which left us all staring at each other in silence. Baker broke it a few seconds later. 'A world class, international art forger that no one had ever caught. That's who we have on the ship.' He turned his face to look at me. 'We never would have had any idea if it weren't for you.'

'Well, let's not celebrate just yet. We have to catch him first. He has twenty or more valuable works of art in his possession and all we know is that he is old.'

'And possibly Canadian,' added Akamu.

'And possibly not,' argued Rick.

'Why bother to say that?' Akamu asked. 'Clearly obvious in my statement that he might be Canadian was the suggestion that he equally might not be.' As the two men took to bickering like they so often did, I stood up and plopped Anna back on the floor. She had curled up and gone to sleep on my lap. I stifled a yawn; the day was already a long one, but I couldn't get to bed yet.

'Are we heading back to your suite?' Baker asked, also standing up. He brushed some lint from his hat and put it back on his head as he moved to the door.

I clipped Anna back onto her lead, the little dog tugging at it instantly to get to the door. 'I need to take Anna outside before I settle her for the night. Then, I guess, yes, back to my suite. We have work to do still and I need to see what Barbie and Jermaine found in their search.' My stomach rumbled and I remembered the food Jermaine had been preparing. I glanced at my watch: forty-five minutes had passed. I should have eaten first and then visited the old detectives. I could have used the time to change my footwear.

I stared at my shoes by the door, but I wasn't going to put them on again. The deck outside would be cold but I would rather have cold feet than clomp around in my uncomfortable high heels again. I hooked them with a couple of fingers on my free hand and tucked my handbag over my shoulder.

'Do you need anything from us?' Rick asked. Both men looked tired.

I shook my head. 'I don't think so. Thank you for tonight. It would not have been possible to track down the forger's identity without you.'

'We don't know his identity,' Akamu pointed out.

It was a valid point but also missing the point. 'I think we know enough. We know what is happening. We know why and I think we will be able to catch him. That's pretty good detective work for two old Hawaiian cops.'

They both took the compliment, Rick popping the caps from two fresh beers so they could chink them at each other in salute. I wished them a good night and followed Baker back out into the passageway.

'Come along, Anna,' I cooed as I led her towards a door to go outside. 'Let's get your business done so I can get back for my supper.' I wasn't keen to go outside but Anna was, propelled perhaps by the need to perform essential duties.

As I opened the door, both Baker and I heard a shout.

Murder

It was a cry of anguish from somewhere outside. Instantly alert, Baker drew his sidearm and slipped around me. 'Stay here, Mrs Fisher. I need to check that out.'

Then he vanished along the deck and out of sight, leaving me shivering lightly against the cool breeze. Anna tugged at her lead, wanting to move. I let her draw me further out onto the deck as she began the process of snuffling around to look for a spot that suited her needs. I let her get on with it, taking the catch off the extendable lead so she could wander off without me having to follow her too closely.

A minute had passed. There was no sign of Baker, but I elected to remain in sight so he could find me when he came back. Jermaine would just fret if I returned without my armed guard.

Suddenly there were hands around my neck. Someone, a man I was sure from the size and strength, had come up behind me and was trying to throttle the life out of me. I bucked and kicked but he pushed me forward until I hit the railing at the edge of the ship and started to push me over it.

He meant to kill me!

I tried to scream but no sound came out; his fingers were digging into my throat to choke off the noise before I could make it. Powerful hands were crushing my larynx and cutting off the flow of blood to my head. Lights were already sparkling in front of my eyes from the lack of oxygen reaching my brain and I knew I was going to pass out soon. When I did, he would throw me over the side, and I would be gone forever.

I clawed feebly at the hands around my throat, but his vicelike grip wasn't going to be broken. Then just as suddenly as he had grabbed me, he let go. My ears were filled with the banging sound of my own oxygen deprived brain, so much so that I couldn't hear anything but I was certain he was about to lift me into the air and the next thing I would feel would be the bitter sting of the cold ocean engulfing me.

I fell to the deck though, my head striking the hard floor with a thump and I saw what had saved me. It was Anna. My tiny little dog was snarling and yapping and had hold of an ankle. I couldn't hear her, there was just a white noise coming from inside my head, but I hadn't passed out and now that my head was at the same level as my feet, my eyes were working again.

I tried to lever myself up, but I was too late to save my dog. As I struggled to get my hands underneath my body, a large hand swept down and grabbed little Anna around her middle. Then, as my hearing returned, I heard her yelp, the sound of her voice trailing into the distance as the man threw her away. The awful sound of a splash ripped at my heart and I screamed in anger and frustration. I wanted to get up and tear at the man that had attacked me. My head was still filled with fluff though, I couldn't make my shaking arms work and the man was going to grab me again any second.

He didn't though; he ran off. Escaping across the deck to vanish back into the structure of the ship, the sound of approaching footsteps reaching my ears as I finally got my hands to work and was able to sit up.

'Mrs Fisher! Are you okay?'

I looked up at Lieutenant Baker, opened my mouth to speak, got a case of the whirlies and had to lower my head again. 'Anna,' I managed.

Suddenly my dog was climbing onto my lap, her tiny paws dripping water onto my dress. I didn't care though, I thought she had gone overboard.

'I found her in a pool. I heard a splash and there was your dog swimming around in the pool.' I hugged her to me, squeezing yet more water from her sopping wet coat. 'What happened, Mrs Fisher?'

'Someone tried to kill me,' I croaked. My throat was sore. I suspected it would be for days, but my head was clearing, and I thought I could stand. Baker offered me a hand as I tried to get up, he was on the radio and calling for help. As I gained my feet, I noticed that he was standing in a puddle of water. It confused me for a moment until I realised the water was coming from him. He was also sopping wet.

He saw me looking. 'Anna couldn't get out of the pool. I think she hit the water quite hard.' He had gone in after her. His face turned serious again. 'Mrs Fisher, who attacked you? Who tried to kill you?'

I shook my head. 'I didn't see him,' my voice was a desperate croak, the words intelligible but it wasn't my voice I was using, at least not a version of it I recognised. 'He grabbed me from behind.' I tried to order my thoughts; to give a concise report that might help. 'He was strong. And tall, I think. He was able to more or less lift me off my feet by my neck.'

'Did he say anything? What was his accent.'

'He didn't speak,' I told him with a tinge of disappointment. Then I looked up at the sound of more footsteps approaching at speed. A team of security officers were heading our way at a run. They were led by a man I didn't recognise but from his insignia I guessed he was the new deputy captain, Commander Yusef.

'Be careful where you stand,' Baker shouted instructions at the approaching team. 'There's blood on the deck.'

'There is?' I croaked. Baker pointed and sure enough, there were drops of fresh blood on the deck a few feet away from me. Baker was standing back so the expanding pool of water spreading out from him wouldn't wash it away. Anna had wounded my attacker, that was the only conclusion I could draw. Her tiny teeth had opened his ankle so if we could work out who it might be, we could probably identify him by a fresh wound to his leg.

Then Anna coughed, a deep hacking noise like she had made earlier when she had a piece of cotton stuck in her throat. Knowing what it might be, I prised her jaws open and peered inside as she fought me. I couldn't see anything in the dim light but fished a finger to the back of her mouth. It made her gag, but I found the problem: another piece of cotton. This time it had a black sequin attached to it.

'Do you have an evidence bag?' I asked, holding a disgusting finger in the air glistening with dog slobber and a piece of soggy cotton.

Commander Yusef barked a command and one of the officers appeared at my side with a small plastic bag. 'Are you alright, Mrs Fisher?' the commander asked, taking a knee next to me.

'How do you know my name?' I asked. We hadn't met yet.

He winked at me; an odd gesture given that we didn't know each other. 'It precedes you.' Sensing that his answer wasn't enough, he added, 'You're an attractive, mature blonde woman with a small red Dachshund and you appear to be right in the thick of things.' It made me irrationally angry for a moment that he was able to identify me from that small subset of descriptors. Then I remembered he had called me attractive and decided to forgive him. 'I was just coming off duty on the bridge when I heard the call. I am glad to make your acquaintance, Mrs Fisher, though I would have preferred to do so under more gentle circumstances.' I couldn't argue with that.

Under his instructions, the security team swabbed the blood and took photographs of the scene. Not that there was a lot to see; there would be no fingerprints to gather, no chance of fibres unless they found one on me. Just in case, the commander wanted to take my dress. I was getting visibly cold, the wet lump held to my chest adding to the cool breeze and he was aware enough to see my need to get inside.

He chose to escort me himself, radioing Alistair as we walked, the commander's jacket around my shoulders to ward off the cold. Despite the attack, my handbag never left my shoulder and my keycard was still in it. Jermaine reacted swiftly to the door opening for once, his face etched with concern which he saw had been warranted the moment I came through the door.

Barbie was on her feet too. 'We called the guys to see what was keeping you. Rick said you just left. What happened?'

Commander Yusef answered as he guided me into the suite's living area. 'Mrs Fisher was attacked by an unknown assailant.'

Jermaine rushed in to take Anna from me. 'I'm okay,' I assured him. I meant it but my croaking voice didn't convince him. 'She's cold. Please get her dry and keep her warm.' I dropped my shoes by the door and let my feet carry me the rest of the way to my bedroom. 'Barbie can you help me, please? They need my dress in case the attacker left DNA or fibres on it.' She was already following me to my bedroom, her hands out in case I needed them to steady myself.

Once inside, she closed the door behind us. 'Are you sure you're okay, Patty. That's some nasty bruising on your throat already.' I nodded rather than speak. I didn't hurt anywhere other than my throat. Where his fingers had dug in was quite sore and I could see what Barbie was talking about when I looked at myself in the mirror. Several purple abrasions were visible on the skin with blotches beneath them. I could expect a hue of colours to appear over the next few days.

I slid out of the dress and handed it to her so she could take it outside to the waiting security officers. Then I found some gym gear, a cotton warm up suit in two parts and a stretchy t-shirt. I also found an underwire bra which was a relief to put on; some support finally. Blessed relief flooded through me as I slipped my feet into a pair of running shoes. It wasn't elegant, but I was more than ready to swap fabulous for comfort.

Barbie came back for me, but I was heading for the door anyway. I had heard Alistair arrive, his concerned voice echoing as he got a report from his deputy. In the living area of my suite were now most of a dozen white uniformed crew including the captain and the deputy captain. Lieutenant Baker was partly dressed, his top half naked as he dried himself. He would be within his rights to call it a night, but it looked like he was swapping his wet uniform for a dry one, determination etched on his face.

'Are you alright, my dear?' asked Alistair, taking me in his arms for a gentle caress. He looked into my eyes, then ducked his head to inspect my neck. 'You have no idea who it was?'

Once again I shook my head, saving my voice as much as I could. 'Anna saved me,' I croaked. The little dog was wrapped in a towel on the couch where one of the security team was patting her head and fussing her ears. She raised an eyebrow at the mention of her name but closed it again in happy contentment as the petting continued. 'Then Baker scared him off.'

Alistair nodded his thanks at the half-dressed man. 'Did you see anything, Baker?'

'No, sir. I think whoever it was, was waiting for us. We heard a shout, like a call for help and I went to investigate, but I think I just fell for their distraction and separated myself from Mrs Fisher so the attack could happen.'

I hadn't thought to ask if he had found anyone when he dashed off to see who had shouted. It made sense to draw the armed guard away if they planned to kill me. Why was I the target though?

'A beverage, madam?' asked Jermaine, offering me a cold glass that must surely contain gin and tonic. I spied the cucumber floating in it and accepted it gratefully. It wouldn't fix my throat but I was going to tell myself it might.

I took a long sip then drifted to a chair. I needed to speak now and everyone was watching me. 'Whoever attacked me, it wasn't Irani. Are we agreed?'

The question was aimed at Alistair and he knew it. 'Agreed. He is still being held in the brig.'

'Exactly. Now, that still doesn't prove that he didn't kill Dayita, but I have more to tell you.' I stopped my next sentence as I thought of something. 'Did you ask him if Dayita was his daughter?'

Alistair met my gaze. 'I did. You were right. Why am I saying that?' he laughed at himself. 'Of course, you were right. Irani Patel had no idea that Dayita was his daughter or even that he had a daughter until she told her mother she landed a job on the show as one of the professional dancers. She told her then and there who her father was after lying about it for years. Dayita approached Irani only a few days ago, taking time to work up the courage to speak to him about it, no doubt. He couldn't work out how to break the news to his wife and still hasn't. He admitted having a panic attack about it right before the show. That's why he was late to arrive and looked sweaty.'

I reached into my handbag to produce the packet of prescription medicine I found earlier in his bathroom. 'Yes. I found his meds.'

Alistair took the packet and read the label. 'Always one step ahead of me. So, I planned to speak with Devrani, I was on my way there when Commander Yusef contacted me about you, but I don't think Irani Patel killed Dayita and that means he didn't kill Rajesh either.'

'Which means we still have a killer on the loose.'

Alistair eyed me strangely. He wasn't the only one in the room to do so. 'I thought that was obvious since someone just tried to kill you?'

I took another sip of my drink. 'That depends on whether it is the same person.' Now I had everyone's attention. 'Everyone is assuming there is only one killer.'

Barbie's hand went to her mouth. 'You think there's more than one?'

'I haven't told you about Freddy the Forger yet.' Of the people in the room, only Baker knew this part of the story. He chose that moment to excuse himself so he could finish getting into his dry uniform, carrying his fresh clothes over one arm as he retreated into a bedroom. Then, with the attention of the room, and much like the old Canadian police officer had, I told the story of the forger and his calling cards, keeping the room silent with the fascinating tale.

When I finished, my drink was empty, and I wanted another. 'That's incredible,' said Alistair slowly. 'Just incredible. The man must be ancient by now though.'

'And he's not the killer so how did his calling cards end up on the two victims?' asked Barbie.

I didn't get to answer though. Around the cabin, the radios attached to the officers' lapels all crackled as one then a voice spoke a code word. 'Secretary. Secretary. Secretary. Deck twelve, elevator bank G. Out.'

The crew members responded as one. A passenger had just been found dead.

Number Three

In the blink of an eye, everyone who had been sitting was on their feet and moving toward the door. Those that hadn't been sitting were already there and going out of it. Poor Baker was hopping through my suite still pulling his trousers up. His top half was covered but not buttoned up and his shoes were tucked under his right arm while his sidearm and its holster were hooked over his head.

I took one look at Jermaine and Barbie and followed everyone else. They followed straight after me. Only Anna stayed behind, raising a single lazy eyelid before closing it again and snuggling into the couch.

At the door, Alistair held up a hand. 'I would rather you didn't come, Patricia.'

'Ha!' I scoffed, squeezing by him and leaving him behind. 'One: fat chance. Two: I'm safer surrounded by all these armed men than I am in my suite so put up with it.' He gave no further argument as we all ran after the security team already tearing along the passageway to the nearest elevator. I didn't know where elevator bank G was but I would find out soon enough.

In the quiet of the steel car as we rode down, Alistair quietly mumbled. 'Lord, I hope it's not another one from the show.'

We got out on deck twelve and hurried through a maze of passageways to get to the right place. It took us more than ten minutes, but the crew knew exactly where they were going. As we arrived, I could see more white uniforms ahead of us. I didn't recognise anyone but the man nearest the captain began to report before we got there. 'One of the passengers reported the elevator malfunctioning, sir. Someone from maintenance went to look at it and found blood coming through a panel in the ceiling.'

'Who is it?' Alistair asked, his voice quiet, but determined and his mouth set with grim acceptance.

'We haven't identified him yet, sir. The engineer is inside the car now. He's going to lower it to the next deck manually so the roof of the car will be at this level.' Just then, a door opened on the other side of the small atrium that housed the elevators and a harassed-looking man in a boiler suit emerged from the door. He had grease spots on his clothing and a rag sticking out of a side pocket on his trousers.

He took in the scene before him, nodded at the captain and strode toward the elevator doors. 'I'll have these open in a jiffy.' He did something to pop a panel open next to the elevator buttons, isolated the electronics that controlled the doors, I know this because he was giving a running commentary, then forced a tool between the doors and pushed them open. He said, 'Urrrrgh.' And stood back, turning his head away from the sight inside.

The security team were less squeamish and filled the gap in front of the open doors as the engineer moved away. They blocked my view but I didn't need to get close to be able to tell that it was indeed another member of the dance show. The sequinned leg I could see through the gap between security officers was sufficient clue in itself. I had a good idea who the leg belonged to as well.

'It's Vihaan Veghale, isn't it?' I asked.

At the leading edge of the lift shaft and crouching to get a closer look, Commander Yusef swung his head around to look at me and then at everyone else. 'I can't tell. Does anyone know them well enough to identify him on sight?'

With a reluctant sigh, I came closer, peering through the mass of bodies as they parted to let me look. Vihaan Veghale looked very dead indeed. His arms were contorted at unnatural angles, the bones inside very clearly broken and his head was a bloody mess. There was no doubt that it was him though and I knew I would find a small wound on his ankle.

'This is the man that attacked me.' I stated.

Commander Yusef's eyes went wide in surprise. 'For heaven's sake, why?'

'Can somebody check his ankles please? One of them will have a small bite mark from my dog.' As Commander Yusef performed the task himself, lifting first one trouser leg and then the other to reveal the wound, I explained what had happened earlier. 'I think this is about sexual preferences and about tolerance in India. I believe Vihaan was homosexual but terrified about the truth coming out. Much the same as we saw with Rajesh earlier this evening, he lived a secret life, associating himself with attractive women and keeping his true sexuality under wraps. I think he worried that I had stumbled onto his secret when I visited his suite earlier.'

'Hold on,' said Alistair wearily. 'Can you back up a bit? Why were you in his suite earlier?'

I paused, gathering my thoughts. Then said, 'No.'

'No?' he questioned.

'Not yet, anyway. I still haven't got all the pieces and I want to explain this once rather than several times. We need to see if he left a suicide note.'

This time Alistair threw his arms in the air in frustration. 'So this is suicide? Not murder? He threw himself down an elevator shaft?'

'I think so?' I tried, hearing the uncertainty in my voice. I genuinely wasn't certain which is why I didn't want to answer a dozen questions right now. 'If there is a note it will be in his room and may explain a good portion of tonight's drama.'

'But you still think he tried to kill you?' Alistair demanded, upset about the fact that I had been attacked but also that I wasn't telling him everything. 'Is he the one that killed Dayita?'

'I don't think so.'

'What about Rajesh?'

'Probably?'

'Probably?' he echoed, his eyebrows matching his disbelief as they tried to climb off the top of his head.

'I think they were lovers.' Just behind and to the side of Alistair, Jermaine nodded his head in agreement. That fit as far as he was concerned.

Alistair gave in arguing. Pointing a finger at different members of his crew. 'Schneider, go with Baker and Mrs Fisher's party. Open up Vihaan Veghale's suite and look for evidence. Bhukari, you stay here to secure the body with Thompson and Van Mogler. Wait for the on-call doctor and try to keep passengers away. I don't want anyone seeing this. Get a cleaning crew to make the elevator sparkle.' He turned toward the engineer. 'Is the elevator broken?'

'Um, no. It shorted out when his face went through the ceiling proximity sensor. It will work perfectly when I get it cleaned up.' I grimaced at his description, but Alistair kept going with his instructions.

When he finished directing the actions of his crew, I asked, 'What are you going to do?'

'I'm heading to the bridge. I'm going to do something I know how to do: captain this ship. Goodness knows I make a poor detective.'

I slipped an arm through his and walked with him. Barbie, Jermaine and the security guys following us as we walked arm in arm back in the direction of the next nearest set of elevators. We only got about two paces though before the stair door opened again and Dr Kim came through it. He exited right in front of us, almost bumping into me as he came into the passageway. 'Captain, Mrs Fisher. In the thick of it again?'

The question was aimed at me, not the captain. I didn't know whether to laugh or cry at my constant involvement in all the onboard tragedy, but he was right. I asked a question of my own though, rather than answer his. 'Dr Kim, you inspected the body of Rajesh Kumar earlier this evening, yes?'

'I did.'

'Was strangulation the cause of death?' Everyone in the small passageway and elevator atrium had paused to listen to his answer.

'It was.'

'Rajesh, like all the male dancers, was strong and muscular, was he not? In your opinion, could a woman have strangled him?'

Dr Kim pursed his lips before he answered. 'That is difficult to say. I certainly wouldn't wish to be quoted, but I would say no. Not unless the woman was exceptionally strong. The hands were gripping him from behind, the fingers digging into the throat. The killer would need to be at least as big if not bigger than the victim. His larynx has been crushed. It would have taken considerable force to do that.'

'What about Irani Patel? Could he have killed Rajesh?'

Dr Kim thought about it but slowly shook his head. 'Probably not. Irani Patel, given his age, probably doesn't possess the strength. Also, Irani is several inches shorter than Rajesh and I believe his killer to be taller.'

I nodded. 'Thank you, Dr Kim. I won't keep you any longer.' As the doctor made his way to the open elevator shaft and the body waiting in it, I started walking again. I was heading to Vihaan's suite and I was certain I would find a suicide note there.

Confession

There was no sense of satisfaction when we got to Vihaan's cabin and found the note he left. It was lengthy, but it explained everything. He even apologised to me in it, begging that I forgive the last desperate act of a desperate man. I found my emotions conflicted. I was sad for him because he had been living a lie for so long, but the depth of my sympathy couldn't extend very far because he had killed Rajesh to hide his lie.

It was all in the note; a complete confession. Rajesh wanted to come out. They had been lovers for some time, but Vihaan wasn't ready for the backlash of public opinion being openly gay would bring. They argued and Rajesh said he was going to do it anyway. Vihaan followed him, cornered him in the gents' toilets where we found him and pretended to agree. They started having sex and Vihaan strangled him.

'This is all very neat,' Baker concluded when he finished reading it for the second time. 'But who killed Dayita?'

Annoyingly, I still didn't know the answer to that question. Vihaan admitted that he had taken the calling card from his suite and used it to shift the blame. He got the idea when he heard about the card found stuck to Dayita's chest. He had already discovered it, knew what it was because he heard Devrani ask Irani for it and genuinely thought that Irani was guilty of killing her. He was happy to shift the blame for both deaths to Irani, but when I came looking for the calling card, he knew I was on to him and tried to eliminate me too.

I rested my weary body in a chair for a moment. At some point soon they would have to assemble the cast and crew of the show and tell them that yet another one of their number had died. When that happened, I wanted to expose the killer. However, in order to do that, I had to get my brain to work out what I had missed. There was a final piece of the puzzle here somewhere, I just hadn't seen it yet.

I knew Irani wasn't the killer, so I had to ask where the card stuck to Dayita's chest could have come from. The obvious answer was that it was the one from Irani's room but since not all of the break ins had been reported and we thus had no way of knowing how many cards had been left so far, it could have come from anywhere. One of the other stars of the show might have found it in their suite, or even picked it up off the floor since Irani appeared to have lost his. That didn't make sense though because we knew all of the stars were accounted for at the time of Dayita's murder. The only person missing had been Irani which was why he looked so likely to be the murderer. All the television crew were likewise accounted for; all busy doing their jobs to make sure a live show went to plan.

Then I caught a glimpse of an idea. I could think of another person who wasn't accounted for, another person that was without an alibi. It hit me like an electric shock, jolting me from my chair and onto my feet, new purpose making me feel energised.

Barbie saw me move and saw my face. 'What is it, Patty?'

'I need to speak to Irani Patel.' I was already reaching for Baker's shoulder. 'Can you get on the radio and find out if they have released him yet?'

I caught him by surprise, but he didn't bother to question why. Then he was clicking the button on his radio and talking to someone at the other end. Call signs and code words bounced back and forward until he said, 'They are just letting him go now.'

'Can they hold him until I get there?'

'Sure. Why?'

'Because he might be guilty after all.'

Final Clue

We could hear Irani arguing the moment we stepped out of the elevator. The brig was an uncomfortably familiar place. Just a few days ago I had been locked up here against my will while I was trying to save everyone on board. Barbie had come to the rescue that time, but I never imagined I would see the place again.

Now here I was, walking voluntarily into the ship's darkest side. That they needed a brig at all was an indication that things did not always go to plan, and they needed a way to be able to contain a person or people while at sea. Irani wasn't necessarily considered dangerous, though if you were to believe he was a murderer, then one might wish to observe some precautions when dealing with him. Whatever the case, his status as a suspect in the murder of Dayita and Rajesh meant that taking him to the brig where he was separated from everyone else was also nothing more than a sensible precaution.

He wasn't happy about it though. 'Ten minutes ago, you were releasing me. Now you want me to wait. Open the door. I tell you I haven't done anything, and I demand to be returned to my suite.'

A calm voice replied. 'I'm sorry, sir. I am not authorised to do that at this time. I cannot tell you why I have been instructed to hold you here, but my understanding is that a party is on their way here now. In fact, I think I hear someone approaching.'

They couldn't see directly into the passageway from the brig, but they had cameras inside which showed them the approaches so they would be able to see who was outside.

As we turned the final corner, two guards came into view, standing outside the entrance to the brig. I cringed as I saw them. They were the same two guys Barbie had tasered and then we had stripped and tasered again as we locked them in their own cells.

I heard Barbie say a bad word under her breath as the first man saw us, nudged his friend and the pair of them moved to block the passageway, their impressive shoulder width all but filling it when they stood side by side.

'Well, look who it is, Raymond,' said one to the other.

Raymond grinned a leering grin. 'Yes, Graham, this is an unexpected pleasure. Barbie the buxom gym bunny, no less.'

Baker lifted a warning hand. 'We don't need any bother, gents. We are here to speak with Mr Patel, not trade wits with you.'

Graham sneered in his face. 'We haven't forgotten your part in it either, Baker.' He raised a finger to prod Baker in the chest. 'The day is coming. There will be a reckoning.' Then he pointed his gaze between the shoulders of Baker and Schneider to look down at Barbie. 'And as for you, blondie...'

'That's it, boys. Goodnight.' The voice came from behind them and belonged to Lieutenant Deepa Bhukari. The instant she said it, Graham stopped talking and started to twitch, his face contorting as spasms wracked his body. Next to him Raymond was doing the same. Then they both pitched forward, Baker and Schneider jumping backwards out of the way, so the two men fell to the deck.

'Wow, those two are annoying,' Bhukari sighed as she opened the cell door to the brig. She had tasered them. Again.

Barbie high-fived her. 'Nice one, girl. What'cha doing down here?'

'The captain sent us down here to make sure Mr Patel was escorted back to his suite. We were just about to leave when Baker came on the radio and asked us to wait.'

'Hi, Mrs Fisher. Hi, Barbie.' Pippin waved a greeting as we went into the brig, stepping over the still twitching forms of Raymond and Graham.

Irani was standing beside him looking impatient with his arms folded over his chest. He looked at me, 'Are you the person that has kept me here? I saw you earlier. Who are you?' But I wasn't looking at him, at least, I wasn't looking at his face. I was looking at his cuffs.

He was clearly expecting me to answer him but I didn't. Instead I crossed the room to get closer to him, staring at his cuffs the whole time. Crossing his arms had pushed the cuffs of his shirt out beyond his jacket sleeves, exposing the cufflinks that would normally be hidden inside if his arms were hanging down.

I could see both cuffs but only one cufflink. 'Mr Patel where is your other cufflink?'

'I don't know,' he snapped irritably. 'I lost it at some point this evening. They were priceless, you know. A gift from the Sultan of Brunei,' he boasted again. 'I performed a play at his palace for his fiftieth birthday. These are the only ones like this in the world.'

'What is it, Patty?' Barbie asked, coming to stand next to me. I hung my head. I was right. I had also been wrong. But I knew who the killer was now, and I knew why Dayita had been killed.

'What? What is it?' demanded Irani Patel. 'What is happening?'

I blew out a breath; I felt tired again, but I could see the end of it now. 'Mr Patel, I know who killed your daughter…'

'Tell me,' he begged. 'Tell me who it was.'

'I promise that I will very soon. We need to get back up to the top deck and we need to assemble the cast and crew of your show.'

'Why can't you tell me now? I demand to know!' he looked angry, but also sad, the weight of the day hanging heavy around his neck.

I offered him an apologetic face. 'I'm sorry, Mr Patel. I will not make you wait very much longer though.' I looked at the security officers. 'I'll see you there?'

'Where are you going, Mrs Fisher?' asked Baker.

'To set a trap.'

The Big Reveal

I had always been a fan of Agatha Christie. Miss Marple was my favourite, the quiet, unassuming know-it-all waited until the very end and then told everyone what had been going on and why. That's what I was about to do but it hadn't come about by design exactly. Nevertheless, the security team were busy asking everyone from the show to assemble back in the ballroom. No doubt Deepika was doing her producer thing and insisting everyone attend. Faced with the possibility that she would be stuck with Taginda as a stand in host, she was likely keen to see me again and see if I could make good on my promise to give Irani Patel back.

With Jermaine and Barbie at my side, I went via a cabin on the eighteenth deck. Jermaine, of course, knocked on the door, stepping in to perform the task so that my precious knuckles would be spared. We had to wait a while; it was after midnight and the occupants had probably been in bed a while. They had been drinking too so it was no surprise when Jermaine stepped back to the door and rapped again.

I could hear grumbling coming from the other side long before it was open and a shaft of light appearing at the bottom of the door as the lights inside came on.

'There had better be a drop-dead gorgeous blonde at the door when I open it,' grumbled the voice on the other side. Barbie quickly shoved her way to the front with a giggle, displacing Jermaine as she placed herself in front of the door with a big smile on her face. 'And she had better be naked,' added Rick as he wrenched the door open.

Barbie's smile froze at his final request and Rick's face coloured. 'Well, half a wish fulfilled is better than none at all,' she said.

'Erm, yup,' He peered around her to look at me as Akamu came lumbering into sight, scratching his belly and yawning. 'Patricia, to what do we owe this particular pleasure? You do know it's the middle of the night?'

'Yeah, it's work time.' I grinned as I put a hand on Rick's shoulder and spun him around. He let me do it, then let me push him back into his cabin.

'What is it this time?' Rick asked with a sigh of acceptance. It was all a big show; they loved that I included them in the adventure. Akamu plonked himself down on the couch and rubbed his eyes to make them work. Rick yawned and scratched at his shorts. I ignored what he was doing until he was ready.

'Shall I make coffee, madam?'

I smiled at my butler. 'Thank you, Jermaine. That will not be necessary. We will not be here long.' Then I told my two retired cop friends what I had realised and what I wanted them to do. Then I handed over my stolen universal keycard and left them to get dressed. They had a job to do and it had the potential to be open ended. I figured I had an hour at the most, but who could tell.

With the time it took to answer their questions and go over the plan twice, I figured the ballroom would be filling up by the time we got there. I was more right than I realised, the sound of the crowd inside telling me most of the cast and crew were already there before I got inside and saw them.

It was well after midnight on a Saturday night, or, if you wish to be pedantic, a Sunday morning and no one looked happy to be rousted from their beds. The ball gowns and sequins were long gone, as were the ornate hair styles and intricate makeup. No one was in their pyjamas or night wear though lots of them had opted for sportswear and few looked ready to do anything other than go back to bed once they found out why they were wanted.

Deepika rushed over to me the moment I came into the room. 'Is he here? Were you right? I need Irani Patel back. If I hear one more demand from Taginda there will be another murder, I swear.'

It was obvious from her statement that Irani hadn't arrived yet, but I scoured the room with my eyes looking for him anyway. Alistair wasn't here yet either, but I had quickly become the centre of attention and people were heading my way.

'Why are we here?' a voice asked.

'What's going on?' from another.

'Who are you to be gathering us?' was perhaps my favourite, but I didn't answer any of them.

I turned to Deepika. 'Deepika, these are your people. This is your show. Irani will be here in a minute, but he is not their leader; you are. They need a steady hand to get them through this.'

'What is this? What has happened now?' Deepika spun around to stare at the crowd of people, trying to work out who might now be missing. 'Is anyone not here?' she called out.

The question stopped everyone in their tracks, all of them looking around at everyone around them, all now trying to work out who was there and who wasn't. Then the questions I had been facing went up a notch in both insistence and volume.

A cry of anguish, 'Where's Anushka!'

'Right behind you dummy.'

'Oh.'

'Where's Kareena?'

'Hold on, where's Vihaan?' urgent voices coming at me from multiple directions, undertones of anger mixed in with the concern.

'Hey, what aren't you telling us?' The faces were pressing closer, mob mentality threatening to bubble over into something unpleasant. Jermaine stepped in front of me to stare them down but there was only one of him and an awful lot of them.

Then one voice cut above all the others. 'What is the meaning of this?' The absolute authority in it made everyone stop. The captain of the ship had arrived and he had an entourage with him which included his deputy, Commander Yusef, half a dozen members of the ship's security team, plus Irani Patel and his wife.

It was show time.

'I thank you for remaining calm, ladies and gentlemen.' Alistair walked into the centre of the room and addressed the assembled television people. Now that he had their attention, he met as many eyes as possible, lingering on some while passing more quickly over others. 'I must also thank you for all for coming at such short notice and at such an ungodly hour. I will not keep you any longer than is necessary. This has been a terrible evening. Despite the success of the show, tragedy has struck. You lost two of your number last night, and I have recently learned that Vihaan Veghale took his own life just a short while ago.' Shocked gasps and yet more cries of surprised anguish came as the inevitable result of his announcement but he pressed on. 'He left a note in which he admitted to murdering Rajesh Kumar.' This time the gasps came accompanied by shouts of denial.

'I'm afraid it's true.' I butted in, moving to stand beside Alistair.

'Who are you?' asked Taginda, the plump Indian woman taking centre stage as soon as she got the chance.

Alistair hit her with a hard stare. 'I have the honour to introduce Patricia Fisher. Patricia is a one of the Aurelia's most valued guests and the one person who has been able to determine what has been happening tonight.'

Taginda screwed up her face. 'You mean, you're sleeping with her. I saw you both sitting next to the judges. Why should we listen to your girlfriend? Where's Devrani? He knows what's what.' She turned around to look for him and found him skulking toward the back of the crowd. 'Hey, Devrani, get up here and tell them why Irani is the killer.' She made urgent gestures to get him moving. I folded my arms and watched to see what he decided to do.

Initially reluctant, he saw no option other than to come forward when the crowd parted in front of him. Taginda clapped him in and whooped like he was a contestant arriving on stage for a game show.

'Irani would you come and join me, please?' I met the show host's eyes and nodded at him, imparting that it was going to be okay. Then, as he came toward me, I held out my hand for him to take. 'Before Devrani Bharma has a chance to confuse you, I need you to know a few things.' I leaned in close to Irani and whispered. 'I have to tell them about your daughter and about your anxiety. Are you ready?'

He gave me an unhappy look and bowed his head but did so with an affirmative nod. With his right hand holding my left, I turned back to

Taginda and the sea of faces staring at me. 'Irani Patel was late to the show this evening because he suffers from anxiety.'

There were a few, 'Whats?' from the audience.

'Sometimes the anxiety gets so bad that he has panic attacks and that was what happened right before the biggest show your nation has ever seen.' Seeing the disbelieving faces staring back at me, I said, 'Does that surprise you? It doesn't surprise me. When Dayita was being murdered, Irani couldn't have perpetrated the crime because he was having a panic attack. That's why he was late and why he looked so sweaty and flustered at the start of the show.'

'Do you have any witnesses to corroborate this?' Devrani asked. He looked more confident now, as if I had just exposed a major flaw in my argument.

'Yeah,' echoed Taginda, getting on his side because it worked in her favour for Irani to be guilty.

I smiled at them both. 'I don't need one.'

'Why don't you need one?' asked Taginda but I didn't bother to answer.

'What I suspect none of you know is that Dayita is Irani's daughter.' My revelation got several shouts of disbelief from the audience and a cry of horror from Mrs Patel. Irani dropped my hand to rush to his wife's side. She looked faint and began to swoon as he got to her. Lieutenant Schneider leant a hand to lower her gently to the floor. 'Neither Irani nor Dayita knew until recently, her father's identity was kept from her by her mother.'

Deepika stared at the Patels. 'That makes perfect sense. That's why you have been sneaking off to see her. It's not just here,' she said to the room. 'I caught him coming out of her room last week at the studio in Mumbai.'

'Why didn't you say anything?' demanded Taginda.

Deepika gave the other woman a hard stare. 'I assumed they were having an affair and it was none of my business.'

'Alright,' said Taginda, aiming her face at me. 'Let's say we believe you and Dayita is Irani's daughter. So what? He could still have murdered her. He was the only one that wasn't around when she was killed and we only have your word for it that he was having a panic attack.'

'Hold on,' the new speaker was Arabella, Vihaan Veghale's dance partner. Her face was a mess of tears and her nose was red from crying but she had a question. 'Irani's wife said they were having sex right before the show. She provided his alibi. Was it a lie because he was having a panic attack and she was covering for him?'

Among everyone present, Arabella was the only one that had remembered mousy, little Mrs Patel. She was a background figure, a near recluse who didn't go out in public and was only here because she wanted to support her husband. That was the story she gave but the truth was that she wanted to keep tabs on him. 'The story of the marital event was a lie, but not one cooked up by Mrs Patel to cover up her husband's panic attack. She knew nothing about it. She wasn't with him.'

The crowd were silent as I moved about, ordering my thoughts so I would get them right. 'Mrs Patel didn't know about her husband's daughter. Like many of you she thought he was having an affair.'

'No! I would never,' Irani protested, holding his wife in his arms as he gazed down at her.

'She came on this trip to spy on him, convinced he was having sex with one of the dancers. She may have come to this suspicion by herself, but I think it more likely one of you tipped her off.' I saw Taginda twitch in surprise and forcibly gather herself again. I had it right. 'I went to Dayita's room this evening not long after she had been murdered. Her room had been trashed; someone had been in there looking for something. For evidence. One of the key pieces of evidence against Irani was the blue opal found in the ladies' bathroom where Dayita was murdered. The opal came from his cufflink and how could it have got there unless he was also there?'

'That's right,' agreed Taginda, ever hopeful.

'I also found a blue opal in Dayita's room, carefully placed beneath a dresser so it would be found but not straight away. The killer was trying to frame Irani.'

'You must be kidding?' scoffed Taginda, turning to Devrani for support. He gave her none though, he was listening to me with the same rapt fascination as everyone else.

'The other key piece of evidence was the calling card found impaled by the knife that killed Dayita. This was less convincing than the opal, but it was known that Irani had found a calling card in his suite this evening and had it on his person. When he couldn't produce it and one was found with Dayita, the case against him started to stack up. No one knew that Dayita was his daughter, you see. Everyone that saw him going into her room assumed they were having an affair. Even the one person that could easily get one of his cufflinks and take the calling card from his pocket without him noticing.' I had them all waiting, and I made them wait. 'The evidence the person was looking for in Dayita's room when they tore it apart this evening wasn't the thing that they found. Oh no. The thing that they found was much worse. Hoping to find evidence of an affair they suspected to be taking place, the killer found a pregnancy test wrapper.' I turned to look directly at the Patels. 'Isn't that right, Mrs Patel?'

Irani stared at me for a second, then looked down at his wife and back at me. 'No,' he argued. I said nothing. 'No, it can't be.'

Mrs Patel was still half lying on the floor and half cradled in her husband's lap. She looked dreadful, the truth of not just her crime but her error hitting home now that she knew what she had done. 'I didn't know!' she wailed. 'I thought you were having an affair and then that little bitch was going to have your child.' Her words came out as hoarse sobs, ragged breaths heaved in between each one.

'Our grandchild, Sheba. It would have been our grandchild. What are you saying, Sheba? Did you do this?' She couldn't answer. She had murdered her husband's illegitimate daughter for jealousy and now she was trying to cling to him in her sea of despair.

Everyone in the room was silent, gawping at the Patels as they sat on the floor. Finally, Irani pushed her away, prising her fingers from around his neck as she refused to let go. Alistair nodded a silent instruction to Baker and Schneider, the two men stepping in to help Mrs Patel up so they could escort her from the room.

'Wait.' The shout came from Taginda. 'Are you sure? Are you sure Irani isn't guilty?'

Deepika had an answer for her, 'Taginda.'

'Yes?'

'You've just been voted off.'

Taginda opened her mouth to argue but a cheer from the rest of the stars and dancers and crew shut her up before she could speak. She gawped at them all, then ran from the room, beating Mrs Patel and her security escort to the door.

Devrani Bharma offered me his hand. 'Well done, Mrs Fisher. Clearly, I underestimated you. I think perhaps too many years of acting the role has dulled my senses.'

'Thank you, Mr Bharma,' I said graciously.

'Tell me though,' he started to ask as Alistair came to my side, 'Where are the calling cards coming from and what is that all about?'

Secret Mission

'I can't hold it forever. I'm not a young man anymore, you know.'

'Yes, Rick, you told me. Can you hold it a few more minutes?'

'That's what you asked me ten minutes ago. Look it won't take me a second. I'll be in and out. If they come in while I'm in there, I'll stop mid-stream and...'

'No,' I insisted. 'You can hold it a little bit longer.' Rick needed to pee and had been complaining about it for half an hour now. His predicament wasn't helped by Akamu who kept making peeing noises or talking about water trickling over rocks.

'Are they always like this?' asked Alistair.

I sighed. 'Pretty much.'

We were hiding in the dark in a suite on the upper deck. Mrs Patel's arrest was little more than an hour old, but it was now after two in the morning and I was genuinely worried I might fall asleep if something didn't happen soon. That Rick was still here was his fault. When we left the ballroom, I sent him a text message to confirm the two of them were still in place, then made my way to them. We were there to replace them, but they wanted to stay and see it through.

On route from the ballroom, I explained my idea to Alistair: we were going to stake out a suite and catch the calling card criminal red handed. I could see that he didn't want to question my theory, but he had to point out, 'You said the pattern had finished so you couldn't predict where he would strike next.'

'That's right.' I offered him no further answer or explanation until he got grumpy and demanded it. In his words, 'If I am going to authorise a sting operation on one of the best suites on my ship and let you use my officers to do it, then I need to know what is happening and why.' I laughed at him and told him what I knew.

When I finished explaining, he said, 'Really? It's that simple?'

'I think so.'

So now we were waiting in the dark, tucked out of the way so the calling card criminal would walk into the suite and once here with the painting in his hands, we would step out and spring the trap.

Rick was right though, I was also beginning to feel the need to move or go to the bathroom or do something other than stand still hidden behind the bedroom door.

Then we heard footsteps approaching down the passageway outside. At this time of night, with so little background noise, sound travelled. They weren't the first footsteps in the last hour, but these ones stopped right outside, breaking the shaft of light coming under the front door. The click of the solenoid signalled the door being unlocked and two sets of footsteps came into the suite.

There was no chatter. They were operating silently, and hidden in a bedroom, I couldn't see them. I knew who they were though. It had come to me suddenly when I was in the brig with Irani. Without Anna for once, no one was getting their ankles bothered which was a relief but was also a habit of hers that had saved my life earlier. Standing in the brig, thinking about ravaged ankles made me glance at Lieutenant Baker's trousers and that was when the spark of light went off inside my head. His trousers weren't ravaged anymore. He had changed them.

By my shoulder, Alistair moved. He couldn't be seen by the people in the main living area but he had direct line of sight across the suite to another bedroom where Baker and Schneider were waiting. He signalled them with a simple hand gesture, then made sure Bhukari and Pippin were also alert behind him, then held up three fingers, folded them down one at a time and stepped out of the bedroom with his side arm raised.

Baker and Schneider did the same and the five white uniforms fanned out to surround the two men in the middle of the room.

I sauntered in after them. 'Good evening, Charlie.'

The old man looked bewildered for a moment and I thought he was going to use the senile trick again, but instead, he smiled and tipped his head back to stare at the ceiling. 'Well done. Patricia, isn't it?' With the weapons still trained on the two men, Baker and Schneider moved in to make sure Charlie and his son were not armed and then insisted they both take a seat on the couch next to each other. Charlie never took his eyes off me. 'How did you do it?'

'It was your stupid need to work patterns, Dad,' snapped his son.

I had to correct him. 'It wasn't, actually. I thought I had you with a pattern yesterday evening, but we were too late. You had already been and that completed the circle so you would be starting a new circle and thus I couldn't predict where you would be.'

'But you did predict it, Patricia,' pointed out Akamu. 'That's how we came to be here.'

I grinned at him and at everyone else. 'No. This isn't the next suite on their pattern.'

The sound of a toilet flushing preceded Rick rejoining us. 'What the heck is it then?'

'It's their suite.'

Charlie raised his hands which made the weapons twitch but all he did was start clapping.

'Oh, stop it, Father,' growled his son.

'I told you I would be bested one day. Didn't I always say, I would be bested.' Charlie looked positively overjoyed at getting caught. 'I have to ask how you did it though.'

'I didn't,' I admitted, which raised even more eyebrows. 'My dog did.' My explanation wasn't helping anyone to see the solution so I sat down on a chair to rest my weary bones and started to talk. 'When I bumped into you at the champagne reception earlier, you had a tear in the ankle of your trousers. I heard it rip and thought I had done it with my shoes.' I looked at Rick and Akamu. 'I was wearing these ridiculous high-heels that I thought I could pull off. Anyway, I felt bad about it but then my dog was hacking on a piece of cotton that was caught in her throat. It was red cotton and you are wearing red socks, aren't you, Charlie?'

With a twinkling eye he lifted a trouser leg to show off his socks. The right one had a snag hanging from it. 'That little dog took a chunk out of me. Vicious little thing it is.'

'Only to those she doesn't know,' I pointed out. 'It took me a while to realise it was you. Your senile act is very convincing. I'm sure it throws a lot of people off the scent.'

'It's a new thing,' he admitted. 'It's only been the last few years I could get away with it.'

While we were talking, Baker and Schneider were inspecting the suite, Schneider popped his head through a bedroom room door. 'Sir, I've found them. Dozens of them. More than we realised.'

I looked at Charlie. 'How many suites have you hit so far?'

'All but two,' he boasted. 'Tomorrow we would have mopped up the last of them and been off the ship in Mumbai. I have buyers waiting. They sure will be disappointed.'

'No doubt,' I agreed. That was that though. There was nothing more to say and plenty more to do. For the crew that is; I had done everything I was going to. It was way after my bedtime, and I was beaten. As I got up, I remembered something though. 'Charlie, I have a question for you.'

'Oh, yes?'

'Many years ago, you were almost caught by a cop in Montreal.'

'That's right,' he replied gamely. 'Frank Tremblay. I remember him well. He is the only one. Until now that is. He was the only one who ever got close.'

'Well, he has a question for you. I think it's been bugging him for decades.' Charlie gave me his full attention as he waited for me to ask it. 'Why did you always steal on a Thursday?'

He laughed, tipping his head back in a deep guffaw. 'That's what he wants to know? Well, I'll tell you. It was soup.'

'Soup?'

'Yup. I got supper after each of my... nocturnal adventures. There was a great place in Montreal that served the best soups. I never could have anything heavy that close to bedtime, but soup was just right. Well, on a Thursday they served the best chicken and asparagus soup. Fresh made but only on a Thursday.'

I took his answer with me, promising to pass it on to the retired Canadian cop the next day. I wondered what he would make of it.

Breakfast in Bed

When I woke in the morning, sunlight was streaming through my window and another glorious day had begun while I snored into my pillow. A small noise of displeasure came from next to my elbow as I moved it and Anna's face appeared. She had a habit of climbing on the bed during the night. Not that it bothered me, she never woke me, I just woke to find her nestled in next to me most days.

She yawned deeply, her jaw opening to a crazy angle only a dog can achieve, then she licked her lips and plopped off the bed. The sound of water being lapped from her bowl told me where she had gone.

Then I heard my bedroom door opening. Anna instantly went into attack mode, barking as she streaked across the room. My latest attacker was ready for her though, using a tray to fend her off as he came in bearing two steaming mugs of tea in his other hand.

'Good morning, Patricia.'

I smiled up at him. 'Good morning, Alistair. I still can't believe you stayed last night.'

He placed my tea on my nightstand and sat on the edge of the bed. 'You solved the crime and won the bet and demanded I spend the night as my forfeit.' Then he leaned in and kissed me. When he broke it a moment later, he said, 'Would you like breakfast in bed?'

I chuckled at him. 'If that's what you want to do.'

He laughed as well. 'I don't think I have ever had breakfast in bed.'

'Well, I'm certain Jermaine will be only too pleased to prepare whatever you fancy.' And that's exactly what he did.

Epilogue:

'Have you got everything you need?'

'Yes, Alistair. I will only be gone three days. You don't need to worry. I have a butler with me for goodness sake. I won't have to think for myself at any point.'

'You're sure now?' he asked for what felt like the fiftieth time.

I swatted his arm. 'Go on now, get back on your ship. It can't sail without you.'

'It won't be the same without you on board, you know.'

I met his gaze. This was one of those serious moments when you have to say the right thing. I took his hand. 'Alistair, you know I get off the ship for good when we reach Southampton. You know that, right?'

'Yes, Patricia.'

'At some point we are going to have to have a conversation about what that means for us and what we want to do about it.'

'If you would like to come back on board, we can talk about it right now.' I wasn't sure if he was joking or not, but I wasn't getting back on board today. I was going to Zangrabar where a Maharaja was waiting to treat me like royalty; his words not mine. His private jet was waiting for us just a few miles away at the Mumbai International Airport. Alistair seemed uncomfortable about letting me go, not that he had any say in the matter, but had convinced me to include two of his security team in my party. There were eight of us in total, spread across two limousines, not the cruise line's limousines though, which would have happily taken us wherever we wanted to go, but super-stretch limousines provided by the Maharaja. I was guessing he wasn't short of a penny or two.

Already in the car and getting into party mode were Rick and Akamu because, come on, I just couldn't leave those two reprobates behind on the ship; they might get up to anything. I chose Baker from the security team because I knew him better than anyone else and Deepa Bhukari because she was good friends with Barbie. Jermaine, my ever-present butler was with me of course, as was Barbie. The eighth member of my entourage was a surprise addition. A surprise for Barbie that is, not me. I had been communicating with the surprise addition in secret for a week so when Barbie came off the ship and found Hideki waiting for her by the limousine, she screamed and danced on the spot, then hugged me and ran off to embrace him. She was sweet on him, that was for sure.

Barbie chose that moment to power down the window and shout for me to hurry up. 'Your gin is getting warm!'

'Well we wouldn't want that,' said Alistair. 'You should go. I don't want you to miss your flight.'

I rolled my eyes. 'I can't miss my flight. It's *my* flight.'

He nodded. He had only been teasing. I kissed him then, in the shade of the great ship and felt odd that it would be sailing the next leg of its perpetual journey without me on it. My home for the last two months would just have to manage without me for a few days though; I was going to visit a country I had never even heard of until I boarded the Aurelia and my life changed.

We broke the kiss and he let me go, watching me as I walked to the car and got in and was still watching when we drove away. I couldn't be sure, but I think he waited until we were out of sight before he turned around.

I breathed out. A heavy sigh that I had been bottling up for a while. Then I turned to Barbie and the other people in the car. 'Where's the damned gin?'

The End

Author Note:

That's the end of Patricia's sixth adventure but as you just read, she's off to Zangrabar where there will most likely be intrigue, adventure, and mystery waiting for her. You can read an extract from that on the following pages.

As I write this personal note, I am sitting at a dining table in a vacation home in Florida. I quit my job just a couple of weeks ago to work on my author career full time. The holiday was booked a year ago though, so right or wrong, we are here and spending money I probably don't have. I expect though that I have nothing to worry about and without the pressure of a full-time career, I can focus of writing full time and get many more of my ideas out of my head and onto paper.

For me this is a dream coming true. No boss, no annoying, lazy staff, but the opportunity to take my son to school or to farm club, to walk the dogs when the sun is above the horizon and to avoid the diabolical pressures that corporate life has brought me.

I return to England in a few days after two weeks of sunshine, Mickey Mouse and water parks. My four-year-old son has had the time of his life and therefore so have I. However, once the laundry is done and my beach shoes have been swapped for wellington boots, it will be time to knuckle down and write. I promise to do what I can to make each book a brilliantly enjoyable romp.

This is not my first series though; there are many other books already waiting for you. So, if you enjoy Patricia's adventures, you may wish to check out **Tempest Michaels**, **Amanda Harper** and **Jane Butterworth**. Like Patricia, they solve mysteries and their stories are written to make you laugh and keep you turning pages when you really ought to be going to sleep.

Finally, there is a **Patricia Fisher** story that you may not yet have found. It is part of this series but sits apart from it. It is called ***Killer Cocktail*** and you can have it for free. Just click the link below and tell me where to send it.

Yes! Send me my FREE Patricia Fisher story!

The Missing Sapphire of Zangrabar
The Kidnapped Bride
The Director's Cut
The Couple in Cabin 2124
Doctor Death
Murder on the Dancefloor
Mission for the Maharaja
A Sleuth and her Dachshund in Athens

The Maltese Parrot
No Place Like Home

Extract from Mission for the Maharaja

Unwelcome Intruder

Ninety minutes later, I was putting in my earrings. It was the last touch for my outfit; one which I had taken my time to pull together. The suite was large and luxurious, and I was utterly alone in it so I had taken my time and run a deep bath. Rick had been exaggerating about being able to do laps in it, but it was big. Certainly, it was the biggest bath I had ever been in but primping and preening and getting myself ready hadn't dispelled the sense of unease I felt one little bit.

Was there something to Aladdin's claims?

A noise from somewhere outside of my bedroom drew my attention. It was the sound of Anna bothering something. Usually the noise she was making came to the accompaniment of someone else swearing as she tore a chunk out of their ankle. No such shouts arose though.

'Anna,' I called, hoping she would come. 'Anna, come on girl.' She didn't appear and the sound of her growling continued. Huffing, I got up but as I did so, she came trotting through the door.

With a large snake in her mouth.

To say I was stunned would really fail to capture the emotion I felt when I realised what she was carrying but that too paled in comparison when she dropped it and I saw that it was not only still alive, but also rather annoyed.

I don't know much about snakes, but I know a cobra when I see one. It raised its head of the floor in a show of defiance, so Anna dived at it, knocking it down with her tiny paws and instinctively gripping it just behind its head so it couldn't bite her.

Then she carried it over to me, proudly prancing with her prize and keen to show it off. I said, 'Arrrrgh!' which wasn't my most articulate sentence ever. However, it managed to capture all of the emotions I felt quite neatly. 'Mummy doesn't want the snake, sweetie,' I insisted as I jumped off the dressing table chair and backed away. Anna kept coming though, desperate to show her human what she found.

She dropped it again, the large snake sensing it was beaten this time and making a bid for freedom by darting under my bed. There was no escape form Anna though, she growled as she ran after it, ducking when the snake tried to strike her, then coming in underneath it to grab its neck once more.

This time, she gave it a good shake, much like a dog does with a chew toy when excited. The snake reacted badly to being vigorously shaken though; it had more moving parts than a stuffed bear, so this time, when she spat it out, it just rolled onto the marble tile and looked dead.

Because it was.

Ever since I kicked Aladdin out, I had been wanting to call Jermaine. I knew he would come running and the chances were he was struggling with the concept of having someone to do things for him. I resisted though because I would be placing my needs before his. Now though, I needed someone to get rid of a snake and no matter what I acknowledged about my life and my spirit changing over the last few weeks, I wasn't picking up the ruddy great serpent just in case it was only pretending to be dead.

With my phone in my shaking hand, I dialled the number for his cell. He picked it up as if he had been waiting for it, 'Madam, how can I help you? Do you require my assistance?'

His response dialled back my panic about twelve notches; just hearing his voice made all the difference. 'Jermaine, angel, you need to stop called me madam. We are very much equals here, even if you argue with me about the concept on the Aurelia. I could do with your assistance though, despite what I just said. I have a dead snake on the floor of my bedroom. A big snake. Is that something you could help me with?'

'I shall be with you momentarily, ma... Mrs Fisher.'

'Try again.'

He sighed deeply before saying, 'I shall be with you momentarily, Patricia.'

'Thank you, Jermaine. I look forward to seeing you.' I clicked the phone off to end the call and looked down to where my Dachshund was still worrying the dead snake. 'Anna, where do you find that?' I asked. I got no answer, of course, just an inquisitive look for a second before she went back to nudging the dead snake with her nose.

A knock at the door broke the spell and jolted me from staring at Anna and the snake. Stifling the need to call out that I was coming, I made my way to the door as swiftly as I could while laughing internally at how slowly Jermaine would have moved it were him answering the door; his determined resistance to hurrying something that always entertained me.

However, when I opened the door to find him in his butler's tails, I could do nothing but sigh. 'You brought the outfit with you?'

He met me with an even gaze. 'I suspected, madam, that it would be needed.' And now I was stuck. A few seconds ago I had pushed him into addressing me by my first name, now he back in his butler's guise and I already knew there was no way he would address me as anything but madam.

I stopped fighting it. 'The snake's in my bedroom.' Jermaine stepped over the threshold and into my suite, one of the few people that could do so without Anna trying to kill them. Not that Anna hadn't tried at the start; she had several goes at ripping Jermaine's ankles to shred but he was fast and he was always so calm. Anna gave up trying to bite him a week ago when she got bored with being scooped into the air and cooed at.

Jermaine needed no further encouragement from me. He nodded once and strode into my suite to deal with the offensive serpent's corpse. I heard a toilet flush and that seemed to be that. I hadn't moved far from the door but I was close enough to hear Jermaine move through my suite and the sound of gas escaping as he opened a bottle. The gas sound was followed by the sound of ice hitting the bottom of a glass and then he reappeared with what was very obviously a gin and tonic in his hand.

Relief washed through me in a surprising way; I hadn't even tasted it yet, but I shot him a raised eyebrow anyway. 'Where's yours?' He opened his mouth to respond, undoubtedly planning to say something butlery, but I shot him down. 'I have no wish to drink alone. Will you join me?' I said it softly; we were friends, even though he liked to pretend our relationship was master and servant.

From behind his back, he produced a second glass and held it up to mine with a smile. Then his lips wobbled and he glanced down and back up, caught in indecision about what he wanted to say. I gave him a second of silence, then stepped into his personal space to place a hand on his arm. He locked eyes with me then and found his voice, 'Thank you for being my friend, Patricia.'

My breath caught in my chest, an involuntary reaction but the honest one nevertheless. Somehow, Jermaine and I had grown very close. He was my butler and acted as if it was an absolute privilege to bring me things, yet I knew he felt the same way about me as I did about him. There was nothing sexual in it, yet it was perhaps the closest relationship I had ever experienced with a man.

I could think of nothing to say, so I raised my glass in a salute and took a sip. It was sublime. Then it hit me. 'Where did you find gin in a dry country?'

'I am not without resources.' A large hip flask appeared in his right hand and disappeared again just as quickly. 'Everyone seemed surprised that this was a dry country; I knew already and never thought to question my need to smuggle something in.'

I sipped my gin, sensing that there might not be many of them to come since our supply was limited. Its cold, deep flavours collided with my taste buds like two cars in a head on crash though I resisted the desire to express my pleasure. Instead, I asked, 'So, what do we do now?'

'We get ready for the banquet, madam. Do you have an outfit selected?'

Banquet

An hour later, with a gin of a strength that could be used to start an engine inside me, I was ready to face my adoring crowd. Except I wasn't. Not really. The whole concept of being worshipped was freaking me out. I could handle a small amount of adoration; a few thank yous, but a banquet thrown by a Maharaja with heads of state from various nations all there to witness my majesty – well, that was too much.

Nevertheless, I was dressed like a fairy-tale princess in the wonderful robes provided for me. They were made of a luxurious silk that was as soft and cool as a cloud against my skin and they made me look like Princess Jasmin from the Disney Aladdin movie. Jermaine had expertly crafted my hair into a weave held in place with jewelled pins, once again provided for the event. The reflection in my mirror wasn't everything I wanted it to be – I was fifty-three now I reminded myself more than once. Still, it wasn't terrible either and my outfit for the night was good enough to cover my midriff, a concern that instantly arose when I saw it laid out for me on the bed.

Jermaine reappeared, letting himself back into my suite having departed to get himself ready. He looked like an Arabian prince; his butler's gard replaced by an ornate black tunic interwoven with gold thread to match gold trousers. 'Are you ready, madam? An honour guard is waiting outside to escort you to the banquet.' Like it or not, it was time to go.

I nodded with a grimace. 'Can't put it off any longer. Are the others ready?'

'I have yet to check, madam.'

I crossed the room to where Anna was asleep on my bed, picked her up for a quick cuddle, then placed her in her own bed rather than have her trying to jump down later when she wanted a drink of water. She would most likely just sleep while I was out. 'Let's knock for them on our way, shall we?'

The others must have had the same idea though because they were knocking on my door before I could get to it. Anna responded in her usual manner, barking and tearing across the marble tile to kill whoever had dared to knock. Barbie's voice cooed back at her through the door, not that it did a thing to calm her down. Jermaine got to my door first, scooping the terror sausage before he opened it.

Outside, were Barbie and Hideki, and Deepa and Martin. Both girls had outfits similar to mine, but they were both happily showing off their taut bellies. They were three decades younger than me, but I still took a moment to grumble internally at the ravages of time. The chaps both wore the same outfit as Jermaine, and each looked a million dollars. Beyond my friends was a six-man honour guard wearing ceremonial robes

'Ready to go?' Deepa asked.

'Any sign of the Hawaiians?' I asked in return, peering along the corridor to see where they were.

'We thought they might be with you,' replied Barbie, her brow wrinkling. 'We got no answer from their doors.'

I shuffled out, my friends outside spreading out to let me get into the passageway while Jermaine followed me and closed the door. Another door opened a little further down the passageway, a couple emerging arm in arm.

'Isn't that the French Prime Minister?' asked Martin, his eyes bugging out of his head a little. Panic swirled around my stomach again; who was I to be getting honoured tonight in front of all these people?

Wanting as many people by my side as possible, I hammered on Rick's door, saying, 'I expect they just fell asleep.' No answer came though and no sound either. Where was his valet? I might have dismissed mine, but surely Rick's would be in attendance.

'Could they have already gone down without us?' asked Deepa. Martin was at Akamu's door and getting as much response from it as I was from Rick's. I shrugged. There was no way of answering the question until we found them.

With no other options, we proceeded without them, following the honour guard along the wide passageway. It was a good thing they came for us though; we would never have found our way without them. Even though the banquet was inside the palace, in a huge room filled with exotic plants and exotic people, it still took ten minutes to walk there. Musicians were playing what I guessed to be traditional Zangrabarian instruments, but the tune, which I recognised to be *Jive Talking* by the Beegees, stopped as my honour guard entered the vast hall. In its place, a fanfare erupted with a blast of deafening noise. Buglers, the same ones I had seen at the airstrip were trumpeting my arrival. It felt quite medieval, but it killed all conversation in the room as all eyes swung my way and spontaneous applause sprang up around the room. Was I supposed to bow?

I could feel my cheeks beginning to glow from all the unwanted attention, but there was no escape now. The clomp, clomp, clomp of the Visir's staff announced his arrival before he emerged from the crowd. 'Good evening, Mrs Fisher,' he said with a broad smile on his face. Then he turned around to face the room. 'Your majesty, Maharaja Zebradim,

Lords and Marshalls of our armed forces, assembled distinguished guests from around the globe, please raise a toast to tonight's most honoured guest, a person without whom we would not be able to hold the coronation tomorrow. I give you Zangrabar's saviour, Mrs Patricia Fisher.'

Many of the people staring at me gave polite applause, but most of those I would pick out as being Zangrabarian nationals, whooped and cheered like we were at a football game and I just scored the winning goal. Then the crowd parted and once again the Maharaja floated toward me on his bed of cushions.

'Mrs Fisher, please join me at the head of the table.' Without uttering a command, the men bearing his bed stopped walking and lowered it to the floor so he could get off. In a fluid motion, he stood up and reached out with his right hand to guide me. The applause continued as I followed him to the grand table.

It wasn't really a table though; it was a low platform with cushions arranged around it for everyone to sit on. I had seen people eating like this on television or in National Geographic magazine, I hadn't ever seen it for myself though. Sitting down for the meal, I was concerned about a number of things: Would my host be polite and engaging or a horny teenage brat? Would I like the food? Would I be expected to make a speech, or would I come face to face with the Queen of Spain and be unable to come up with anything sensible to say?

All those concerns vanished though when I realised I still hadn't seen Rick and Akamu. Where were they? I leaned forward to stare down the length of the table. It was arranged in a horseshoe shape with two legs and a top table with the Maharaja in the centre and me to his right.

'Is everything alright, my dear?' asked a man to my right as he too took his seat. When I looked up at him, he said, 'Lord Edgar Postlewaite at your service, ma'am. I'm the British Ambassador in these here parts.' Lord Postlewaite was nearing sixty, his high breeding resulting in a weak chin, watery eyes and a bald scalp. He had a nice smile though.

I glanced at him but only briefly, I was still scouring the assembled persons for any sign of my two missing friends. 'Some of my friends are missing,' I muttered, craning my neck to see. 'I haven't seen them since we arrived a few hours ago.'

The ambassador swivelled his head, which summoned a young man in a suit to his side without the need for verbal communication. He spoke to him though I didn't hear what he said, and the man hurried away. 'Jared will investigate, my dear. Now,' he turned to give me his full attention, 'tell me all about the giant sapphire and how it was that you came to have it in your possession.'

The question was overheard by more than a dozen people sitting in close proximity, so, yet again, focus swung to me, expectation palpable. I didn't feel like I had any choice but to tell the story now, but the young Maharaja made it impossible for me to do anything else. 'Yes, Mrs Fisher. Please entertain me and my guests. I am sure everyone is truly curious to hear your tale.'

I swallowed and took a sip of water to wet my dry mouth, cursed that there was no gin and smiled at my audience as I took them back to the morning I found Jack Langley dead in his cabin. Food was served while I talked, course after course of exotic breads, pastries, sweet fruit teas and more. I didn't get to eat any of it because I was talking, but I managed to fill a plate that I could tuck into when I got to the end.

Further down the table, people were still talking but as I continued, more and more of them fell silent and moved toward me, dragging their cushions with them so they could hear what I was saying. I got to the end and jumped forward to the part where the telegram arrived because it provided a neat conclusion. '...and that is how I come to be here today. I stress the point that recovering the sapphire was a team effort though. Miss Barbara Berkeley, Mr Jermaine Clarke and Mr Martin Baker all played key roles in solving the mystery. I could not have done it without them.'

As I fell silent and reached for my glass of water again, rapturous applause erupted, embarrassing me again. Hoping that everyone would now see I was eating and thus not ask me questions, I selected a flatbread coated in a spicy couscous and popped it in my mouth.

The ambassador leaned in to speak to me as the applause subsided, 'That was quite incredible, my dear. And you told the story with such passion.' Then he placed his left hand on my upper thigh beneath the table and I almost spat out my food.

He saw my reaction and removed his hand. 'Too soon? My apologies, Mrs Fisher, I'm afraid I am finding it hard to control myself. You are quite the filly, you see, and it has been a long time since I last met an eligible English woman.'

A filly? I pierced him with a hard stare. 'Well you can consider me ineligible, thank you very much. I shall thank you for keeping your hands to yourself from now on.'

My rebuke only seemed to encourage him though. 'Yowzer!' he growled, making a noise like a tiger. 'So feisty. I shall do my best to keep up.'

My mouth dropped open as I prepared to berate him for not listening, then chose a different option and turned to speak to the Maharaja instead, giving the ambassador my back. 'Your Majesty, I have a question for you if you would be so kind.'

His attention had been on the crowd in the room, surveying his subjects and honoured guests but he looked at me as I drew his focus. 'Of course, Mrs Fisher. I shall do my best to answer.'

Reminding myself that I was speaking to the ruler of an entire nation and not a teenage boy, I formed the question in my head. Then I saw him glance at my boobs and just asked it anyway. 'In the telegram I received, it suggested you had a mystery you wished me to look into while I am here. I asked the Visir about it, but he didn't know.'

The young king looked worried for a moment, his eyes flaring as if startled or caught in a lie and I felt a twinge of panic myself as I thought I might have somehow insulted him. The emotion passed from his face almost instantly though, gone as if it were never there. 'I'm sorry, Mrs Fisher. That need has been resolved,' he replied with a contented smile. 'Thank you for your kind offer. My only desire for your stay here is that you feel the gratitude of Zangrabar and leave us knowing that you will always be welcome back.'

I bowed my head at his kind words.

Before I could look back up, he clapped his hands together twice, drawing the attention of a hundred servants, the master of the ceremony and most of the guests. 'It is time for merriment!' he shouted loudly and sprang to his feet as musicians began playing once more.

Large curtains to my right, which I believed were hiding nothing more than a wall, swept aside to reveal another vast room. This one was filled with dancing girls, men juggling flaming torches and all manner of other exotica to entice and delight. The Maharaja extended his hand to me, inviting me to go with him as the master of ceremony called everyone else to join us for the night's festivities.

I let the young Maharaja lead me through to the other room, but I spared a glance back at the banquet table; it was still covered in food and all around were confused faces, wondering what had just happened. Dinner wasn't finished. I wasn't even sure all the food had even been served yet but the ruler of the country had decreed that the formal part of the evening was over, so it was.

The back of my skull gave an itch: there was something screwy going on.

Author Note:

That's the end of this teaser from the next story but you can get the full book by clicking the link below. And don't miss the free short story on the following pages – Zombie Granny is from the Blue Moon files, my first series of mysteries but is just as cozy as my Patricia stories and once again stars Dachshunds in a major role.

Mission for the Maharaja

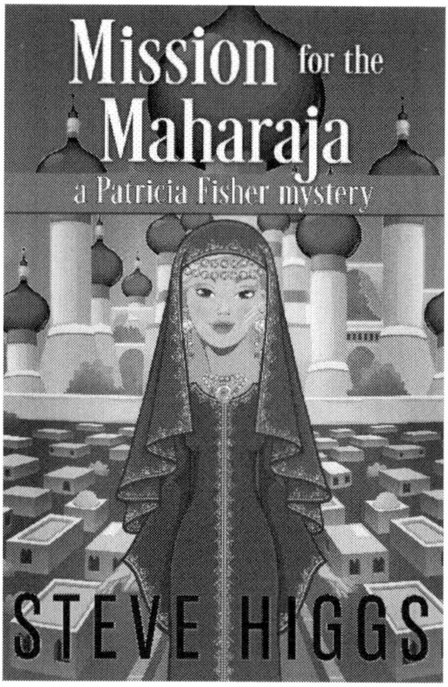
Mission for the
Maharaja
a Patricia Fisher mystery
STEVE HIGGS

Zombie Granny

Blue Moon Investigations

A Short Story

Steve Higgs

Text Copyright © 2017 Steven J Higgs

Publisher: Steve Higgs

The right of Steve Higgs to be identified as authors of the Work has been asserted by him in accordance with the Copyright, Designs and Patents Act 1988

All rights reserved.

The book is copyright material and must not be copied, reproduced, transferred, distributed, leased, licensed or publicly performed or used in any way except as specifically permitted in writing by the publishers, as allowed under the terms and conditions under which it was purchased or as strictly permitted by applicable copyright law. Any unauthorised distribution or use of this text may be a direct infringement of the author's and publisher's rights and those responsible may be liable in law accordingly.

'Zombie Granny' is a work of fiction. Names, characters, businesses, organisations, places, events and incidents either are the product of the author's imagination or are used fictitiously. Any resemblance to actual persons, living, dead or undead, events or locations is entirely coincidental.

Rochester High Street - Saturday 23rd October 1155hrs

I was on my way back to the office when my phone rang. The car system picked it up, the screen advising that the caller was James, my newly employed and very LGBT admin assistant.

'Good afternoon, James.'

'Tempest, I have a client at the office, will you be long?'

'About another five minutes. What sort of case is it?' I was asking if he considered it a real case i.e. there was a crime to investigate or mystery to solve or was the case a questionable one. I got a lot of the latter. Just yesterday a rather well-spoken lady wanted me to help rid her of a plague of gnomes that were ruining her lawn. It's *definitely* not moles she assured me. I didn't take the case.

'It is to do with the zombies.' James continued, excitement in his voice. When I first met James, he was part of a vampire-wannabe cult and I was still trying to convince him that everything supernatural was a load of baloney.

'James, we have been through this several times now. Do you remember what we agreed?'

'Erm.' He started. 'That there are no genuine cases, because there is no supernatural or paranormal and all the creatures like werewolves and vampires and pixies do not exist.'

'That's right, James. That is the entire premise of the business for which you work.'

'But isn't there some actual evidence to support the notion that the zombie legend, which was spawned by slaves in Haiti as they were worked to death by the French colonists, has some scientific grounding. Also, is it not true that the tetrodotoxin poison from the pufferfish can, in sub-lethal doses be used to create a state of suspended animation whereupon the person can be controlled?'

I said nothing for a few seconds, 'James, are you reading to me from Wikipedia?'

'Little bit.'

'Make some tea. I will be there soon.' I was supposed to be a private investigator available for hire to solve crimes, but a young lady at the paper that ran my first advert had misread my business and I had been marketed as a paranormal investigator. The phone had been in a constant state of agitation ever since, so perhaps I should be grateful to her. I was, however, regularly asked to investigate stupid nonsense. A recent case I took on started with the client claiming that her neighbour was a shape shifter - it turned out he was a cross dresser and entitled to be left alone. Another one, that thankfully I was bright enough to turn down, was from a man that assured me he had been cursed by his ex-wife and his todger no longer worked. Occasionally there was a genuine crime beneath the strange circumstances, but the more regular explanation was that the client was daft.

This would be my first zombie case, but I should have seen it coming. The first report of a zombie attack had occurred three days ago in Sevenoaks, a large village with a postcode price-tag high enough to warrant Ferrari opening a dealership there. The zombies had appeared just after lunchtime on a Thursday. They had attacked several shoppers in the village centre. The television and radio had gone crazy with various experts giving their thoughts on what had caused the outbreak.

The second and third incidents had occurred the following day, one in Gillingham and one in Canterbury, but not simultaneously. In all three cases, the number of zombies appearing was limited to a handful, but they were still wreaking havoc. In each case the ensuing panic appeared to have caused several local businesses to catch fire. I had watched the news last night where footage taken on a teenager's phone had been played. In the clip, which lasted about thirty seconds, a little old lady with a perfectly set, pastel-pink perm and matching coat had lunged directly at the phone. Her facial features were contorted, her eyes were utterly deranged, and a deep, guttural sound emanated from the back of her throat.

The footage had gone viral within a few hours, so the world was now talking about *zombie grandma*. She had lunged for and bitten the arm of a pretty teenage-girl. The girl screamed, but then realised that nothing much was happening as the little old lady simply gnawed at the sleeve of her jacket. Another bystander, a boy, shoved the old lady away and she tripped, fell backwards and landed hard on the pavement behind her. The camera zoomed in on the girl's arm where a top set of dentures were embedded. The chap holding the camera had been laughing uncontrollably as the girl screamed in disgust and shook her arm.

On the floor, the old lady was now beginning to cry in pain and was no longer making zombie noises. The news report claimed that she had broken her hip in the fall. The police had arrested her, I think mostly because they did not know what else to do and she had gone to hospital, restrained, and accompanied by several police officers. The report went on to show the Police at the scene where a spokesperson was surrounded by continuous camera flashes which illuminated the early evening gloom. Reading from what I assumed was a hastily prepared statement, he advised the microphones positioned beneath his chin that several persons displaying, as yet, unexplained violent behaviour had been detained for their own safety and that of the general populace. Also, several people had been bitten and admitted to hospital. He refused to engage on many of the rapidly fired questions, which all carried the same theme of whether this was, in fact, the start of a zombie plague.

I had watched the news with greater attention than I had ever given it. I was firmly in the camp that there was no paranormal explanation to anything. Zombies fell into this classification, but the footage was compelling and difficult to argue with. When the first attack had been reported, I had immediately labelled it as a hoax, perpetrated by actors.

What else could it be?

Now though I was not so sure. If it was actors, then they were really committed to the role. I had just taken on an additional investigator, Amanda Harper. She was a police officer and was still working out her notice period before coming to the business full time. This meant I had someone who could tell me what the media would not, so I knew the police has set up several special holding areas where they were still keeping the zombies they had already rounded up. She was able to confirm that they remained violently aggressive and kept trying to bite anyone that came near them. They showed no interest in food or water or anything else, but the police had been able to take identification from a few of them so now knew they had an eclectic mix of people. It included a primary school teacher, a lawyer, a truck driver, a single mum etcetera. Amanda had appeared genuinely scared when I spoke to her.

I parked around the back of my office and ran up the stairs to find James and an elderly gentleman sat in the two seats near the window that overlooks Rochester High Street. The client appeared to be at least seventy years old. He wore an ill-fitting grey suit that hung on his shrunken frame. His face was a map of thin, red lines surrounding sad and tired eyes. I introduced myself to quickly learn that he was the husband of the *zombie granny*.

The conversation was swift. The poor chap had not been allowed to see his wife nor speak with her since the incident. I understood that she was a key element to the police though. She was the only person who had been acting like a zombie and no longer was. He begged me to investigate what was going on and prove his wife was not a crazed creature lusting after human flesh and I accepted the case. He offered me his life savings, his house, whatever it took but I offered to do it for free. This was not something I had ever done before, but he looked like he had little money and I genuinely wanted to help.

The little old man departed, shuffling down the stairs from my office wearing a brave face. I sat down to arrange my thoughts.

James was hovering behind me. 'Do you have plans for the afternoon?' I asked. He only worked part time hours, six mornings a week.

'Actually, yes. I am seeing a hypnotist.' He paused, waiting for me to show signs of interest. When I did not, he pressed on anyway. 'So, I went to a show with some friends last week and I was hypnotised. Apparently, I have just the right type of mind for it…'

A bit weak and easily led then.

'…and I have been invited along to a special event today.' I continued to show no interest. 'No one else got invited.' His tone was pleading for me to make a comment.

I gave in and asked a question, 'Where is the event?'

He brightened instantly, 'Oh, it's just around the corner in The Casino Nightclub. I had better be off. I don't want to be late.' He grabbed his coat and scarf, bid me a pleasant weekend and headed out the door with a quick goodbye.

Amanda had emailed me a file last night which I had briefly inspected. The file listed the names of the zombies they had been able to identify thus far and provided interview notes from zombie grandma, whose real name was Edna Goodbridge. It also contained other notes they had been able to compile about the attacks, such as time and location of sightings, number of zombies involved and lots of other facts that did not seem all that helpful.

Edna had been treated for the pain and for her broken hip. Her age was recorded as seventy-two. The interview notes revealed almost nothing worthwhile. She had no memory of how she came to be in Sevenoaks. The previous evening she gone out for dinner with friends in Rainham town centre and had no memory beyond that. There was a line towards the end of the notes that caught my attention. The hospital reported that there were some traces of an unknown drug in her blood. They had sent it off for analysis. I filed the information away for future reference.

I started to make notes. An hour of intense Google searches later and I knew a lot more about zombies than I ever had and knew just about everything the police knew about the zombie appearances during the last few days. I stared at the handwritten pages, flicked a couple of them and reluctantly admitted that it meant *nothing*.

I scratched my head and made a cup of tea. *Ok. Let's try this from a different angle. If the people acting as zombies are not actually zombies, but are also not consciously playing at being them, then what are they? How does a person arrive at a state where they believe they are a zombie when they are not?*

I was stood next to the window idly stirring my tea when a possibility just popped into my head: *hypnotism.*

Could that work?

Galvanised into action, I dumped the tea, grabbed my jacket and ran around the corner to the occult bookshop owned by Frank Decaux. Frank was a connoisseur of all the weird stuff that I knew nothing about. He would be able to offer a unique perspective on what might be happening.

Bursting through his door I startled him, and he dropped an armful of gear he was carrying. It spilled over the floor, so I bent to help him pick it up. The first item I touched had its label towards me.

Zombie repellent.

I held it up, 'Really, Frank?'

'I can barely keep it on the shelf, Tempest. All the apocalypse protection gear is in high demand at the moment.'

'Okay.' I said to end that line of conversation. 'I need to ask you about hypnotism and whether it could be used to transform an audience into a zombie army?'

He stared at me incredulously, I had his attention.

'Well...'

'The short version please.' I pleaded. Frank had a habit of telling the listener the history, back story, origin story, alternate theories and how much he was selling books related to the subject for.

'Well, a good hypnotist can make a person do anything. These are real zombies though, Tempest. You must see that.' Frank would believe a paranormal explanation first every time.

I ignored him. 'How long would the hypnotic state last?'

'Well, I believe it depends on the individual. Some people are very hard to hypnotise because they resist the commands, but others could be placed into a hypnotic state perpetually I suppose. Alternatively, they could be triggered to act in a certain way by use of a code word until they were given a different one to revert back to their normal selves.'

I opened my mouth to ask a question, but it died on my lips as a scream from outside pierced the peaceful Saturday lunchtime. Frank and I froze and stared at each other for a brief moment, then sprang into action. We dropped the goods we were holding and rushed to the window. In the street below ought to be a scene of people sitting peacefully in cafés while others with places to go passed by and tourists or visitors poked around in shops. Instead, we were witness to a scene where almost everyone was now stationary. In the café windows, the faces were all looking out through the window rather than across the table at a companion. A base dread was forming a tight ball in my stomach. As I watched, I saw a man in the café get up from his seat and move towards the window to gain a better view. His seat tipped over backwards, but too distracted, he failed to even react as it slammed against the floor.

Then, like a switch being flipped, everyone started moving again. *In utter panic.*

I threw myself away from the window, across the bookstore and out into the street. The bookstore opened into a narrow side street so the main route through Rochester was to my left. In the aperture ahead of me, people were running by, all heading in the same direction. I reached the High Street and turned against the flow, towards the direction the people were running from.

Frank skidded to a halt behind me. I wanted to ask what he thought he was doing, but he had every right to be in the street with me. Despite the terror that gripped his face, I knew from recent experience that he had the heart of a lion. 'Ready?' I asked.

In answer, he showed me a back pack full of anti-zombie gear. The cans of zombie repellent surrounded several tubes of zombie bite relief cream, zombie armour, which was nothing more than shoulder pads, knee pads, and shin guards but spray painted black, some duct tape, heavy duty gloves and one item which I just had to take a closer look at. It was a small, black club with a handle, but it was the name written down the side in neon letters that had caught my attention

Zombie Twatting Stick.

I went to put it back, then changed my mind. I hefted it and swung it a couple of times. If I needed it, I assured myself. *Only* if I needed it.

Less than a minute had passed since we had heard the first scream and people were still charging down the street towards us.

'Get outta here.' A chap yelled to us as he went by us. I turned to see him go but we were already forgotten. Various screams, cries and questions regarding lost family members were audible over the general din.

I was angry. People were scared. This was my town, where I lived. It was no longer some report on television. I intended to find the people behind this mess and punch them. Hard.

Approaching down the street towards me were two people. I mentally re-classified them as zombies because I did not know what else I could call them. They were all classic-movie, shuffling feet, arms stretched out in front of them uttering a groaning, growling noise. One was a middle-aged man in a suit and tie, his slightly greying hair a little mussed and he had blood on his face. I could not tell if it was his or someone else's.

'Come on, Frank. Let's go introduce ourselves.' I suggested as I set off toward the pair.

He locked his eyes on us and drawled, 'Braiiinnns.'

His companion was a petite lady in her very early twenties or maybe younger. She wore no jacket against the cool October air and her stretchy top had been ripped so that her right, bra-clad boob poked out through the gap in the fabric.

She made a grab for a woman rushing by her and managed to snag her pony tail. Then she was all about trying to bite the poor woman.

Dashing forward, I used my zombie twatting stick to break the hot zombie chick's grip. Pony tail now free, the woman fled screaming and was gone. Frank meanwhile had pulled a can of anti-zombie spray from his backpack, fumbled to get the lid off and was spraying it at the zombie business guy in front of him.

It was silly string.

Having lost her prey the hot zombie chick had turned her attention to me. However, she weighed less than I can bicep curl, so I was keeping her at bay with one arm while dragging her towards Frank and the pack of gear. I was going to have to deal with zombie business guy first though.

'Behave.' I instructed hot zombie chick as she tried yet again to bend her neck enough to bite my arm. Zombie business guy lunged at Frank, but there was now so much silly string on his face it was obscuring his vision. If it bothered him, he showed no sign and made no attempt to remove it. Frank side stepped neatly and extended a foot to trip him.

Zombie business guy pitched forward, arms flailing and crashed down in a heap next to the bag of gear. Frank pounced on his back, pulling a wicked looking blade from his belt.

'Woah!' I yelled, still struggling with hot zombie chick. Frank was lifting his arms, preparing to drive the knife into the back of the man's head.

'Cut off the head or destroy the brain. It is the only way to kill them.' His voice a panicked shout.

His arms reached the apex of the swing and plunged downwards. I shoved hot zombie chick away and kicked Frank directly in his rib-cage. The blade missed its intended target and struck the pavement where it lodged between two cobblestones. I snatched it from his grip.

'Frank, they may look like zombies, they are behaving like zombies, but they are just plain, vanilla people under some kind of hypnotic spell.'

He stared at me, shocked that I had hit him and his gaze incredulous because I had prevented his first zombie kill. 'Look,' I said, grabbing hot zombie chick again before she could resume trying to bite me. 'Do zombies have a pulse? Check his pulse.'

It was a simple instruction and Frank placed his left hand on zombie business dude's neck. His face flushed with shock as his fingers felt the steady pump of blood beneath warm skin.

He nodded at me, confirming he understood. 'Duct tape.' I said simply and scooped two rolls from the discarded backpack. A few moments later, our two zombies had their hands taped securely behind their backs, their ankles bound, and several laps of tape had been wound around their heads and across their mouths. We manoeuvred them into a recessed shop doorway and left them. They both continued shaking their heads and wriggling to get free.

While we had been binding them, I had explained my very loose theory to Frank. My hypothesis was that if a hypnotist could induce a state where they acted as zombies and would continue to do so until they were given a code word, or in the case of the zombie granny, given such a shock that they were brought back from their reverie, then that was what we were witnessing. I further hypothesised that the drug found in Edna's blood was going to be the tetrodotoxin stuff that James had been talking about earlier or some derivative thereof. This was either how he got them into the state to induce such a deep hypnosis or how he kept them there. I was stretching, I knew it. However, it was the only idea I had. The only question that remained was *why*?

With our two zombies immobile and the crowd of people in the previously busy street now thinning, I hooked the backpack over my shoulder and set off down the road toward The Casino Nightclub where I hoped to find some answers. I did not ask Frank to come along, I had no wish to place him or anyone else in danger, but I expected he would follow me anyway. He did.

'Is there a plan?' He asked as we began to meet with smoke. I could not see the origin of it but remembered the news report saying that fires had been started at the previous zombie attack sites.

'The plan is...' I started to explain but I failed to finish as a zombie crashed through a store front window to my right and grabbed me. The zombie was a strong, athletic, twenty-something guy who was taller and heavier than me and had caught me by surprise. I went down underneath him, toppled by his momentum, my right arm and the zombie twatting stick it held pinned beneath me and my left arm in his grip. He bit into my shoulder. Even with three layers on it still hurt and I started to see the benefit of the zombie armour Frank had placed in the back pack.

I flipped and shoved him away and managed to slide my arm out from underneath me. Athlete zombie's teeth lost their purchase as I did, however he just lunged for my face and would have bitten a chunk right out of me had I not shoved the end of the twatting stick directly into his open mouth. Frank grabbed his shoulders in a bid to wrestle him away from me and between us we managed to get me out from beneath the man. I was still trying to avoid hurting him, convinced as I was that he was just some bloke that had been drugged and hypnotised.

'Grab the duct tape!' I yelled to Frank.

'We might need a plan B.' Frank said, lifting the pack and backing away.

I turned to see what he was looking at. Six more zombies coming right at us, shuffling and groaning and looking hungry.

Bugger.

My intention to avoid hurting anyone was looking doubtful. Accepting it, I rolled away from athlete zombie and kicked him hard in the side of the head as I went. Noble concept abandoned, my new plan was to survive.

'Frank, find a weapon. This is about to get real.' I shouted to psyche myself up.

I lifted the zombie twatting stick, ready to use it as Frank appeared beside me with a katana. 'Dammit Frank, No.' I screeched. 'These are fake, hypnotised zombies. You can't kill them. Injuries will be hard enough to explain to them when they come around. Put the sheath on it and bash them with it. Okay?'

'Yes. Yes, of course.' He mumbled, somewhat embarrassed by his own bravado. Then they were upon us. With weapons to hit them, they were easy enough to put down but there were more coming. The smoke swirled, shrouding us like a thick cloak, caught between the buildings on a breezeless day. In the last five minutes we had barely progressed down the road towards the Casino Nightclub and the lack of advancement was beginning to annoy me.

'We need to get to the nightclub, Frank. They don't move fast, so we are going to charge through them. Right?'

'Okay.' He replied, clearly nervous and trying hard to ignore it.

Not bothering to offer any further explanation, I steeled myself to charge through the line of zombies that came at us. I grabbed the shoulder of Frank's jacket, so I would not lose him, then broke into a sprint.

Then stopped.

Stumbling towards me from the smoke was James. There were maybe another ten zombies around him, some ahead, some behind but all coming towards us as we were the only people remaining in the street. Everyone else had fled. He was stumbling along in the group, arms out and groaning like the rest. Where the zombies' eyes were deranged though, his were just terrified. He spotted me and risked a wry smile.

He was faking!

The zombies were upon us again, so I hit the first one over the head as gently as one can with a wooden club, then ducked into the lunge of the next one and whacked him under the chin.

'James!' I yelled. 'Crouch down.'

He looked confused but obeyed the instruction. I still had one hand on Frank's jacket in fear of being split up. 'OK, Frank. Let's go!' I found myself yelling again. What can I say? It was an exciting situation.

At a charge, we closed the distance to James, knocking zombies over like pins as we went. It proved to be much, much easier than trying to knock them out without hurting them. Frank and I scooped an arm each without even slowing down and we were running down the road with James between us, his heels dragging along the concrete

More smoke swirled around us and I spotted fire behind a window as flames were licking at the woodwork inside. Sirens could be heard in the distance; police and fire brigade and probably paramedics. All were needed.

Suddenly, the smoke cleared, we were just metres from the Casino Nightclub entrance and there were no zombies in sight. I dragged James and Frank through the open door of the Victoria and Eagle pub to get us off the street. Checking that nobody, and no zombies were inside, I slammed the door behind us. It felt slightly safer for a moment.

'What is going on?' James asked between deep breaths.

Now that we had at least a few seconds to re-group I had questions for him. 'James did the hypnotist create the zombies?'

'Yeah! He did!' He replied, astounded. 'How did you know?'

'Lucky guess.' I said rather than waste time on conversation. 'Next question. How are you not affected?'

'Oh. Well, when we arrived, the chap had an assistant lady and she was handing out canapes. She was very insistent that everyone have one, but it smelled like fish and since I am a vegan, I faked putting it in my mouth and slipped it into my pocket instead. Here it is.' He announced producing a rather fancy, but now sadly battered blini looking object, with a leaf, a blob of something edible and a shake of spice over the top.

'Thank you.' I said, taking the canape and placing it into a little bag I had pulled from one of my many pockets. An investigator keeps things like that just in case evidence pops up. 'Then what?'

'The Great Howsini asked everyone to sit and launched into his show. It was weird though, not like his usual act and I noticed that everyone around me had stopped moving. It was like they were unconscious, but their eyes were still wide open. The weirdest thing was that he was telling them all that they were the walking dead, the most terrifying zombie creatures that needed to feed on human flesh. I was scared because they were all starting to groan and make growling noises, so I played along. The assistant lady threw open the doors and he sent us all out to *kill, kill, kill*. That was what he said, "*Kill, kill, kill!*"

Right then. 'Gents you can come with me if you want, but you may be safer staying here. The Great Howsini is about to learn the error of his ways.' I was going to find this idiot and punch him in the pants. Bring zombies to my town, real or not and you pay for it. The problem being, that I had no idea how to find him.

'James do you have a picture of him, or can you describe him?' I was hoping he was going to be easy to spot and that I could catch him here. If not, I would catch up to him later, but by then the adrenalin would be out of my system, I would be thinking with more reason and would find it far harder to justify hurting him.

'No need really.' James said. 'That's him over there.' He pointed.

Across the street, a man in a suit that screamed *stage show act* with its sequinned seam up the trouser leg and overly long jacket tails, was carrying heavy sacks towards the car park. He was in his late thirties, a good fifty pounds overweight and had very little hair left. What there was formed a black ring around the sides and back of his scalp. The effect making his scalp look like a round mountain rising above particularly dark clouds. Behind him, a woman of similar age and figure was weighed down by more sacks. I pulled out my camera and started filming. Then, I handed it to James with the simple instruction to keep it rolling.

The Great Howsini's real name was Dave Gough. The lady was his wife, Brenda. She was a chemist. Once cornered, they had given in immediately and confessed their story to the police that had arrived on the scene moments later. I was getting to be known by the local police as my job had a habit of landing me in the vicinity of dubious events. But for once, they had skipped over the bit where they arrested me and had allowed me to remain at the scene. The Goughs were caught red-handed with bags of cash and goods stolen from shops, bars and restaurants that they had subsequently set ablaze in order to cover their tracks. Missing money and goods would be discovered at the other zombie attack sites when the ash was sifted.

James's original research into how to make a zombie had been bang on the money. Brenda was a chemist by trade and could legally obtain the tetrodotoxin which she had made it into a drug that would render a person ingesting it in a state of semi-suspended animation. Full of ego, she had bragged how deliciously complex it had been.

The police had departed with the Goughs in cuffs and we trudged wearily back through a desolated and partly destroyed Rochester High Street. We passed fire brigade teams putting out fires and we paused at my office to lock up, and at Frank's bookshop, where we found the door wide open, but the contents unmolested.

I was bitten, battered, bruised and tired, but also somehow elated. It was time for a cold one and I was buying.

The End

Now that you have read this short story and know the flavour of my writing, you can make a more informed choice about investing in more of them. Tempest has a wide and varied group of friends that dip into and out of his stories as he tackles vampires, ghosts, evil Klowns and other foul creatures in his battle to solve his clients' mysteries. A second series of books run parallel with Tempest's stories, overlapping and intertwining - The Harper Files starring Amanda Harper. If you care to read the reviews on Amazon you will find the trend claims all the stories are unputdownable, filled with believable characters in unbelievable situations and funny enough to give you a hernia.

If you want to try some more, you can get the origin story for this series for **FREE**. If you want it, you need only ask. Please click the link below and tell me where to send it. Here's the link:

Yes, please! Send me my FREE story!

Blue Moon Investigations
Paranormal Nonsense
The Phantom of Barker Mill
Amanda Harper Paranormal Detective
The Klowns of Kent
Dead Pirates of Cawsand
In the Doodoo With Voodoo
The Witches of East Malling
Crop Circles, Cows and Crazy Aliens
Whispers in the Rigging
Bloodlust Blonde – a short story

Paws of the Yeti

Under a Blue Moon – an Origin Story

Night Work

Made in United States
Orlando, FL
27 April 2024